THE DITCHED BLONDE

Also by Harold Adams

THE
DITCHED
BLONDE

A Carl Wilcox Mystery

HAROLD ADAMS

WALKER AND COMPANY
NEW YORK

All the characters and events portrayed in this work are fictitious.
First published in the United States of America in 1995 by
Walker Publishing Company, Inc.;
first paperback edition published in 1998.

Published simultaneously in Canada by Thomas Allen & Son Canada,
Limited, Markham, Ontario

Library of Congress Cataloging-in-Publication Data
Adams, Harold, 1923–
The ditched blonde / Harold Adams.
p.   cm.
"A Carl Wilcox mystery."
ISBN 0-8027-3263-1
1. Wilcox, Carl (Fictitious character)—Fiction.   2. Private
investigators—North Dakota—Fiction.   3. North Dakota—Fiction.
I. Title
PS3551.D367D58   1995
813′.54—dc20   95-11743
CIP
ISBN 8-8027-7555-1 (paperback)

Printed in the United States of America
2 4 6 8 10 9 7 5 3 1

For Frank Dingee, a friend for over fifty years, Eldon Stevens, almost as long, and Gordon Andreasen, even longer and sorely missed.

THE DITCHED BLONDE

1

H E W A S Y O U N G , quick, and mean drunk. His first swing caught me ducking, clipped my noggin, split my ear, and splattered us both with blood. As he moved in I slipped under and jerked my head into his jaw. It gave me a second free and I hooked him twice, low, then high. He went down. Slowly he got to his knees and struggled to stand. Before I could plant him again the husky town cop grabbed my arm and hauled me out of the dance hall.

That was my first evening in Greenhill, S.D., population 3,182.

I'd spent the early afternoon painting signs on the Coverly Grocery Store windows while the owner's fourteen-year-old daughter hung around trying to get educated. She was a straw blonde, a little plump and a lot sassy.

She wanted to know why a man lived on the road and painted dumb sings for not much money. I hadn't had much luck making a case for myself and to make up for it overdid reports on the places seen and the people met.

She took all that in with a skeptical stare and said, "What you are, is a sort of upper-class bum."

"So what're you?" I asked.

"Not much," she admitted. "I'm a good student, a rotten cook, and not a bad dancer. You going to stay for the dance tonight?"

"I'll stay, but I'm not much of a dancer."

"I suppose you're more like a beer drinker."

"I play pool too."

"I bet you're good at that, huh?"

"Not bad."

She grinned. I put finishing touches on the sign, cleaned my brush, and wiped it dry.

"Are you going to go get drunk now?" she asked.

"You've about driven me to it."

"Actually, you'd ought to buy me an ice cream soda."

"Why?"

"Because I told my dad I saw you painting a sign on the hardware window this morning and said we ought to get one. That's how come he hired you."

"He might not like me treating you."

"He won't mind. Nothing can spoil my appetite and you can't do anything bad with me in a soda fountain."

"Won't people talk?"

"Oh sure." She said that with great satisfaction.

It was some after four when we went up two steps into the soda joint, took seats at a small round table, and ordered. She had a strawberry soda, I took a chocolate malt. The proprietor, a tall balding gink, looked me over and collected on delivery. He didn't so much as glance at my young partner and I guessed maybe he'd seen more of her than he cared for.

I asked if she got a commission on sales she brought to the place and she thought that was very funny.

She said her name was Steffi, short for Stephanie.

"My father's name is Stephen," she explained, "and he wanted a boy of course but hasn't got any. There's just me and my older sister, Holly. She was born on Christmas."

"How long ago?"

"Twenty-one. Still too young for you, I guess."

"Not married?"

"Nope. She teaches school in Aberdeen."

"She comes home for the summers?"

"Uh-huh. Doesn't like it. Says Greenhill's a hick town."

"What's she do on Saturday nights?"

"Usually a movie. She doesn't like the dance hall."

Three girls Steffi's age came in, saw us, took a table on the opposite side of the room, and huddled, giggling. Steffi ignored them.

"Mr. Hilstrom, who runs the drugstore, told me you were a cop in Corden and caught a killer," she said. "He claims you solved lots of killings. Is that a lie?"

"It stretches things. I was a sub cop awhile and helped out on a couple cases."

"We had a murder once," she said. That came out sounding casually proud.

"When?"

"Well, it was quite a while ago. Maybe four years."

"Tell me about it."

"It happened to Genevieve, a friend of Holly's. When they were in high school together. She was run over by a car."

"How do you know it wasn't an accident?"

"Well, nobody knows why she was out there where she was, by the cemetery west of town. And she was run over twice or more."

"She have a boyfriend?"

"Lots of them. She was real popular. Not as pretty as Holly but fellows liked her because she had such a nice personality and lots of pep and loved necking."

Movement by the front door caught my eye and I glanced up at a tall, slender woman walking toward us. The hair was about the same as Steffi's except longer and more golden. There was no resemblance in the eyes or mouth, but I guessed from the disapproving expression that this was Holly, her sister.

"Did she con you into treating her?" she asked me.

I looked at Steffi. "Was it a con?"

"Sure. Holly doesn't like sodas but she'll take a Coke."

I looked toward the geriatric soda clerk, who raised his eyebrows at Holly. She nodded and he moved toward the Coke spigot.

"I was telling him about Genevieve," Steffi told her sister as she sat down. "He used to be a cop."

"I guessed," said Holly. She folded slender hands on the tabletop and looked at her sister thoughtfully.

I didn't know whether she guessed I was a cop or that Steffi was telling about her murdered friend.

"What do you teach?" I asked.

Holly shifted her cool gaze from her sister to me.

"Sometimes very little. But I try hard with the fifth grade in Garfield School at Aberdeen. Father says you're from Corden. Do you know Fanchon Forsythe? She teaches fourth grade there."

I said I'd heard of but never met the lady.

"She seems to have heard a great deal about you."

I couldn't think of a safe response.

She smiled. It was a knowing smile that no doubt made her small students nervous.

"Fanchon says you've become quite famous as a detective in Corden and towns nearby."

I hoped that was all I was famous for.

"Did Stephanie's story interest you?" she asked.

I admitted it had.

"It was murder, you know. A girl doesn't get run over twice out by a lonely cemetery in the middle of the night just by accident. And there are other details about the case that make it plain she was killed to keep her from talking."

"She'd been raped," said Steffi.

"Not necessarily. But she'd been made love to."

"Was she pregnant?" I asked.

"Ah," she said, "there's the nub of it."

Then she told me the number one boyfriend was in town for the summer and would be at the dance and why didn't I come around and see what I could dig up?

"I'll introduce you," she offered.

That was how I got my ear split.

2

"WHAT BROUGHT IT on?" asked Officer Schoop while the doc was taping up my ear. He'd explained when he got me out of the dance hall that he wasn't worried about the fight, he just didn't want blood all over the floor because somebody might slip on it and get hurt.

The answer to his question would be quite a few things, like the fact my partner in the punching objected to my dancing with a Greenhill girl, my being a snoop, and probably even being alive.

"I guess he didn't like my looks," I said.

"Uh-huh. That coming right after you'd been dancing with Holly would figure. He's got ideas about her."

"Were you the cop when Genevieve was killed?"

"Uh-huh. And I tell you true, if I wasn't old and slow I'd be tempted to smack you myself for bringing it up." The words came in a growl and his busy eyebrows made his scowl gorilla fierce.

The doc put away his tape, told me to take it easy, and suggested I not go back to drinking and dancing. "You'd be best off in bed."

I paid him half what I'd earned all day and went outside with Schoop. Farmers were beginning to leave town in their Model Ts and Chevies and there was a minor bustle along the street east of the dance hall where the restaurant, bar, and pool hall were getting their last business before everything closed down at midnight.

"You got a room at Foster's?" he asked.

"No. Got a tent on a farm west of town."

He nodded thoughtfully and asked if I wanted to make his rounds with him.

"Sure, if you don't think it'll cause any strain."

The scowl eased; he said we'd never tell the doc and we started off.

At the end of Commerce Avenue we stopped and stood under a streetlamp at the corner. Moths, beetles, and a mess of smaller bugs flew around, batting themselves against the white globe above us.

"Gen was found in the morning," he said. "All mangled in a little clump in the ditch. Doc figured she'd been dead since around eleven or twelve P.M. She'd been making love and was about three and a half months pregnant. Rex Tobler, the guy who split your ear, had been dating her most but he was off to Aberdeen that weekend, visiting a friend named Dewey Dutro. I questioned Dutro and he swears they were together that night, drinking whiskey and playing cribbage. Rex admitted he and Gen had been into heavy petting now and again but claimed they'd never gone all the way. He wouldn't believe she was knocked up."

He talked slowly and as if it hurt. Almost as if she'd been his daughter.

"Gen related to you?" I asked.

"No, but I knew her. Everybody knew and liked her. She was special."

"Her parents still in town?"

"Oh sure. Her pa works for the gas company. Probably retire in a year or so. Ma's big with the church, sings in the choir."

"Any other kids?"

"Had a boy. Died of flu in France during the war. They're not a lucky family."

"Holly said her friend had a lot of guys interested—any suspects there?"

"Sure. Tobler was number one but had his alibi. Then there was Mutt O'Keefe—his real name's Matthew but he's always called Mutt—he took her to the junior prom and always danced with her Saturday nights no matter who took her there. His old man runs the local paper—a weekly. Our favorite Catholic. Then there's Jim Baltz. Pa's a farmer but Jim's never wanted any farming and got jobs in town clear back when he was in high school. Smart boy. Moved to Aberdeen soon's he graduated."

"Either of them claim they'd made her?"

He glanced at me, frowning. "No."

"Think they lied?"

"Maybe. Word got out too soon that she was pregnant, so they wouldn't be likely to admit it if they'd got into her. You might expect some girls in town'd at least hint she was putting out to the guys chasing her—it'd be natural they'd be jealous— but I never heard a whisper of that. These young ones keep things to themselves. Don't let us in."

He talked more about the townspeople in general, mostly proper folk who admired puritan traits but pretty regularly did as they pleased when they got the notion.

Just before midnight we walked back to the dance hall and watched while the band played "Good Night Ladies," and the crowd began to flow out into the quiet night. Only the café was still open after that. Couples that didn't go to the café strolled down the dark streets away from downtown and small groups gathered for a time on street corners, talking, laughing, and clowning around. Finally the town was still and deserted.

I walked with Officer Schoop along an avenue running south and slightly downhill. He pointed out homes of a few select citizens, making special note of the Tobler place, which stood on a corner lot surrounded by a wrought-iron fence. The house was light brown, almost gold, with a full attic, gabled windows, and white pillars on the porch.

"Al built that near fifteen years ago. Got an architect from the cities, brought in his own carpenters, and they put it up in jig time I'll tell you. That was back just before he ran for governor and nearly made it."

"What business is he in?"

"Owns the Ford garage and sales."

After we'd admired the mansion, Schoop turned to look across the street and pointed out the second house from the corner. It was a cottage with only one floor and a box porch.

"That's where Genevieve lived. She used to baby-sit the little Tobler girl and sometimes helped with washings and in the kitchen when they had big parties."

I wondered what the parents thought about their son messing around with a servant but decided not to ask Schoop.

"Was the doc able to tell if the girl'd been hit by the car or just run over?" I asked.

"He guessed just run over. More'n once."

"Any tire tracks?"

"Not you could identify—too damned dry around there. If she was flat on the ground the car probably didn't get any dents and the damage to Gen was all inside—I mean—there was no blood spattered around."

We walked slowly back toward City Hall and stood by the front door. I rolled a smoke and lit up. He watched in silence for a few seconds and cleared his throat.

"You, uh, got any more jobs lined up?" he asked.

I shook my head.

"Maybe I could come up with something."

"That'd be fine—but why?"

"Give us some time to talk a little more, get you acquainted with things."

"It's not likely I'd do any good. The killing was a long time ago—you know the people better than I do—"

"Maybe a fella not too close to it'd be able to see things different. I'll tell you, that thing grates on me. It's been doing it for four goddamn years and I'm sick of it. I get you some honest work that'll pay and at least we can take a shot at it. I don't give a damn if it costs me the job. I got to try."

I said I'd be glad to give it a try but wondered, as I headed for the Foster Hotel, who he thought would be after his job for trying to solve a murder.

3

I'D PITCHED MY tent beside the Model T under a cotton-wood on the Allison farm just west of town. Old man Allison had given me free rent in exchange for my painting his name on his mailbox by the road. We both figured we got a bargain. The tree was next to a potato field and when I got up on Monday morning and made a breakfast of coffee, bacon, and a fried egg, I could look across the field toward his house nearly a quarter mile away.

All my gear, the gas stove, utensils, food and water, fitted into the box I built on the Ford's right running board. The cover was hinged and when opened it made a table just big enough for a man who didn't cook up too many dishes.

While I was cleaning up after breakfast, a Buick wheeled down the road from town, parked in the tall grass nearby, and a plump dude eased out of the car and walked close.

I said good morning. He nodded, looked over my layout, and nodded again.

"Neat," he said.

I didn't see any argument in that and waited.

"I hear you're a sign painter," he said. "We need some for our streets. What's your rate?"

"Street signs," I told him, "need two coats of sizing, both sides, not just where the lettering goes. Then it depends on the lettering. Like Cottonwood Avenue's going to cost more than Elm Street."

"I can see that—but it'd be simpler to work out like an average and have a flat rate per sign."

"Sounds good."

"How about a dollar and a quarter a sign?"

"More like a dollar seventy-five."

"One fifty or forget it."

"You got to give me a place to work, then."

"You can do it in the hall over the fire station."

"Is it hot?"

"I'll furnish a fan."

"Okay."

He offered me his chubby hand, we shook, and he said his name was Sullivan. Jack. No relation to the fighter. And he told me my name, which didn't come as a surprise. He drove back to town in his polished black Buick and I trailed in my dusty Model T. In City Hall I showed him my letters book and he picked sans serif, upper case, bold. I didn't tell him it was a good choice; being the man he was he didn't need any bum tossing him sweet talk. I didn't have to ask what his job was. The sign on the door we went through said Mayor's Office and he took the chair behind the big desk in the corner.

When everything was agreed on he sat back and frowned at me.

"What you do on your own time's your business," he said. "But if you're smart you won't worry about Officer Schoop's obsession too much."

I gave him my innocent dumb look, which comes easy but didn't impress him any.

"I know Schoop told you about that old business of Genevieve Sinclair. He's honest enough to have told me why he wanted you in town, but he was smart enough to check out your talents first before talking to me about having you do our signs."

"When'd he do that?"

"Before he went off duty this morning he called Corden, talked with Joey Paxton. They work the same hours. So we got a clean bill on you, as a sign painter and a part-time detective. All I want is you keep your nose clean, don't mess with our young girls, fight with our local boys, or stir up important citizens."

"I already broke a couple of those rules."

"I know. Just don't do it again."

"You want me to set up the signs?"

"Just paint them. We have city people who'll put them in place."

"Who're the important citizens I'm not supposed to rile?"

"The Tobler family, for one. They got more heat than they needed when the murder was new, they don't need any more now since the boy checked out clean."

I guessed *clean* was about his favorite word.

Before leaving I asked if any of the three guys who'd been dating Genevieve owned a car. He doubted it.

"Any of them able to borrow one from a relative or friend?"

"Rex used his pa's now and again. I'm not sure whether the Baltzes or O'Keefes had cars. Suppose O'Keefe almost had to."

"I see why the Toblers might be edgy," I said.

He scowled and told me to buy what supplies I needed and have the merchants bill City Hall. He also told me who to buy from and where they were located. The buying didn't take long and was painless since I never had to open my wallet. Neither the hardware man nor the lumberyard boss asked any questions but where should they deliver the sizing and wood for the signs.

An old-timer who did janitor work for the mayor showed me up to the hall over the fire station and delivered the list of street names and numbers. His name was McGinty. He was bent, skinny, bright-eyed as a jaybird, and curious as a cat. He wanted to know where I came from, how come I was a sign painter, and what were they paying me for the job.

I told him I came from Corden, was lucky enough to know a man when I was young who taught me the painting business, and my pay was good enough to make it worth doing.

"Everybody's talking about you decking Rex Tobler," he said. "Hasn't happened since he was little."

"It wasn't much of a scrap, Schoop stopped it quick."

"From what they say, it was lucky for Rex. I guess you're pretty handy."

"The mayor said he'd get me a fan for this place," I said, looking around the stuffy hall. The only windows were in the front half of the room, which I guessed was about forty by sixty feet. McGinty said not to worry and opened one of the windows with some effort. He tried one across from it and it wouldn't budge. I could see it had been painted in and figured I could work it loose with my putty knife.

McGinty brought sawhorses and boards for me to set up my production line and before noon I was putting sizing on the pieces that would be signs.

I went to lunch at the Do Drop Inn. The owner, Maribelle, was fat as my old man's cook at the Wilcox Hotel, but not as big. Her grin ranged from wide to wider. She welcomed me to Greenhill, urged me to have the hot pork sandwich, and asked how I liked her sign out front. Since it had been done by my old friend Larry I could tell her honestly it was great and didn't even try to convince her it needed touching up.

By midafternoon I was still slapping white sizing on the signboards in the hall over the fire station when McGinty came around and asked was it hot enough for me. Maybe that was because I was down to my undershirt and sweating even though I'd managed to get the stuck window open. It didn't do any good because the wind was from the south and the windows faced east and west.

I told him how hot it was and he cackled a little.

"You ain't really seen anything yet, comes to heat," he said.

I put down my brush and built a cigarette.

"Something tells me you're not talking about weather," I said.

"You got things stirred up like a bear in a bee's nest."

I had a little trouble picturing that but thought I got the intent.

"Who's flustered?"

"Old man Tobler's been at the mayor and the town cop both. He figures you been brought in to pick on his boy and he tried to bring charges against you for last night's fight. It didn't take because the cop was right there in the dance hall and saw everything, but old Tobler figures you were just there to egg him into a scrap. Claims you loosened two of Rex's teeth and maybe caused a concussion."

I suggested we go have a cup of coffee and he was starting for the stairs before I got my shirt on.

We took a booth far from the counter and I asked him to fill me in on the town politics.

He said that'd take a long time. So I said start now then, I'll probably only be in town a couple weeks.

"Well, like you know, Sullivan's kingpin right now. Been mayor two years and figures to make it permanent. Tobler's always backed Phil Nordstrom. He owns the furniture store and the undertaking parlor and is probably the only Catholic in town any of these Scandehoovian Lutherans'd vote for. He ran against Sullivan in the last election and lost by a whisker."

"Sullivan's Lutheran?"

"Congregational."

"An Orangeman."

"No less."

"More of the same."

"Sullivan doesn't seem Irish to me. No sense of humor."

"Oh, he's got a sense of humor all right. No Orangeman without one could ever dream of being mayor in a Scandehoovian town like this. The whole notion's a joke."

"He told me not to offend Tobler."

He cackled again. "And you don't think he knows a joke? He figured right off that'd get your Irish up."

"What makes you think I'm Irish?"

"Oh, you may not be pure, but you've got it. Black Irish. You can't miss 'em. Never pass up a fight, never win a war."

"I'm in a war?"

"Oh yes, laddie, believe me. Dead center."

4

BEFORE DINNER I decided on a swim to clean off my day's sweat and I drove over to a lake two and a half miles west of Greenhill. I planned a bare dip but like every other lake in the territory in those years, this one had gone down enough so there was beach a half a block before water and no way to be sure my nakedness wouldn't offend. I dug up a pair of trunks and went in like a gentleman.

There was a fine spot near the original shore where a whopping cottonwood had blown over and I made a fire in its shelter and cooked hamburgers from meat and buns I'd bought at the grocery before leaving town.

After getting stuffed and having coffee with a fresh-rolled cigarette, I stretched out on the grass and admired the clear blue sky awhile before driving back to my tent on Allison's farm.

It was getting on toward dusk as I sighted smoke over my campsite and guessed what had happened before I was close enough to know it for sure. Somebody had dumped gasoline on my tent and tossed a match inside.

I walked around, searching for signs of my well-wisher, and of course there was nothing. Back in the Ford I headed toward

Allison's place. He was pissed that somebody'd done such a thing on his property but said he hadn't seen anybody around and I believed him.

I found Schoop in his office at City Hall. He was madder than Allison and insisted on going back out to look the site over and kept cussing as he drove.

"If some asshole thinks this'll stop the investigation, he's goddamn gonna learn different!"

"It wasn't just maybe Rex getting back for our fracas Saturday night?"

He thought about that a little and granted it could be the case. He didn't find any more evidence on the scene than I had and we drove back to town.

"This gives me a little problem," I told him. "I haven't got money for a new tarp, let alone a new tent, and my bedroll's gone. You think I can jack some money out of the mayor?"

"We'll see," he said, and headed for the man's house.

Sullivan took the story in without any evident anger or even sorrow. He asked how many signs I'd finished my first day. I said I spent a lot of it just sizing them—probably hadn't actually painted more than eight.

He said okay, he would credit me with twelve dollars and guarantee one week's room rent at the Foster Hotel. That probably wouldn't be more than five or six dollars. He'd loan me the remaining seven or six out of his pocket and deduct the amount from my first week's payment next Monday.

Then he told me if I hadn't been off loafing at the lake the loss wouldn't have occurred.

My first reaction was to get nasty about his not sending me the fan he'd promised but while I was bitching about that it dawned he'd just shown he was as interested as Schoop in the murder of Genevieve.

I cut off my squawking and gave him my kindly smile—the one that always made my old man splutter—and asked if he really expected me to paint signs twelve hours a day.

His broad brow wrinkled a second, showing his self-annoyance for giving me that opening and he waved his soft hand, dismissing my crack. While we sat before his desk he called the Foster Hotel and arranged a week's lodging for five bucks. After hanging up he counted out seven dollars from his black wallet and had me sign a receipt for it.

Schoop walked over to Foster's with me and I asked him what the mayor's interest might be in the Genevieve murder.

He fumbled a couple seconds before deciding there was no point in lying and said old man Tobler was a big man with the Republican party and had always opposed Sullivan from every angle.

"He's satisfied Rex Tobler's the one that'll have the most problems if this murder gets dug up so he'd like to see you working on it."

"Why hire me to do the signs when the murder's what he's after?"

He gave me a disgusted look.

"You need that laid out?"

I didn't.

There was no one in the lobby of the Foster Hotel but a teenager who reminded me of my nephew Hank. Maybe not as good looking. He greeted the town cop politely and studied me close as I signed the register.

It was an even sorrier place than the Wilcox Hotel. There was no dining room and just two beat-up overstuffed chairs in corners opposite the registration desk, which ran across the west end. The boy took in my ditty bag with a disapproving eye and told me my room was third on the left straight down the hall upstairs. Schoop waited while I went up to check it out.

It was a little more pleasant than a cell since there were no bars and the toilet down the hall beat a bucket in the room. The single window gave me a dandy view of a dusty alley and a dilapidated gray bungalow with a junky backyard.

I joined Schoop who didn't bother to ask how I liked it and we stood a moment on the sidewalk, taking in the quiet evening.

"Where'd I have a chance to run cross Mutt O'Keefe natural like?" I asked.

"He never misses a dance, but there isn't one till Wednesday night when they have the old-time shindig. Now and again he plays pool."

"Does Tobler?"

"Afraid so."

"Guess I'll drift over to the parlor."

He started to move with me and I told him as nice as I could it didn't seem a good idea. We talked about it some and finally he agreed to leave me on my own but didn't like it.

There were a couple guys playing at a table near the room's center and a half a dozen more characters watching. Schoop had described Mutt as a red-haired Irishman with a snub nose and tough chin. I thought the hair was more sandy than red and agreed about the chin. He was solidly built, about my height but heavier by a good twelve pounds. His opponent was a skinny kid with thin floppy hair and pimples. Rex Tobler wasn't in sight.

Mutt's game was good enough to win but only by a shade and he kidded the boy while they retrieved the dropped balls and racked them up again. One of the watchers said something to Mutt, who turned and looked at me. I nodded at him.

"Want a game?" he asked.

I moved to the rack, took a cue, and he offered me the break. I left him an easy shot with the one ball, which he dropped casually. His next shot got him nothing and left me little. There was no talk while we played on. I won light. He paid off and suggested another game. I said I'd rather buy him a beer and talk.

He thought that over about half a second and we went up front and took a table.

"I hear," he said after his first swig, "you're in town to dig up old troubles."

"That bother you?"

"No. I'd like to know who did Gen."

"Who do you think?"

"No idea, and that's a fact."

"Okay. Can we talk about the girl a little?"

"We never went all the way if that's your first question."

"If you had and knew she was pregnant, what'd you have done?"

"Married her, and darned glad to."

"No reason you couldn't have, or wouldn'ta wanted to?"

"Not a one. Well, I'll admit I didn't have the kind of job a married man should—but most guys I've known never let that stop them. Especially when the girl was expecting."

"You have any idea back then that somebody was going all the way with her?"

"No. I can't really believe it yet. She was a great snuggler but she set limits. No action below the belt."

"Yours or hers?"

"That's right."

"You figure she was a tease?"

"No more than most. Well, she kissed a lot hotter than any other girl I never necked with. You know, open-mouth style. It got me fired up awful."

"You and Rex Tobler or Jim Baltz ever fight over her?"

"Naw. What the hell, she got to choose, we weren't like tomcats fighting for her."

"And she chose Rex most?"

"I wouldn't say it was that clear. Jim took her out about as often and she was always glad to dance with me."

"And there was nobody else?"

"Hell, there was everybody else. Well, not that much, but I mean, she never let any of us figure she was ours."

"Anybody involved that had a car?"

"Rex got to use his old man's a lot and once in a while Jim got the family half-ton truck. My folks didn't have a car."

"Did any of you guys neck out at the cemetery?"

"None I know. Most girls wouldn't stand for it. Too spooky."

I asked him what kind of a student Genevieve had been and he said good.

"She was always a teacher's pet."

"What was she good in?"

"English, history, math. You name it."

"Who was her favorite teacher?"

"Oh, she liked Miz Whelan real well, and Mr. Galbraith."

"You had a man teacher?"

"Sure. Galbraith taught English and history, and coached the football team. He was a lousy coach but pretty good in English."

I asked if Galbraith were still around and he said sure, he had an apartment next to Foster's Hotel. During the summer he sold farm equipment for a company in Sioux Falls and traveled a lot.

Back to the hotel I found a chubby old woman at the registration counter who told me she had a message from Mr. Tobler. He asked that I give him a call.

There was a pay phone in a little booth off the lobby and I shot a nickel and the operator rang the man, who answered after the third ring.

"Ah yes," he said when I identified myself. "Would you be kind enough to come around to my house? I can offer you a drink and we can chat."

"About what?"

"Oh, several things, your travels, painting signs, and maybe murder?"

I said I'd be around.

5

AL TOBLER ANSWERED my knock and loomed in the doorway behind the screen. In the vague shadows he resembled his son, Rex, but when he shoved the screen open and waved me in I found he was taller and the face was sharper with high cheekbones and a hard jawline. He led me through the vestibule into a large, dimly lit living room. Everything in the place was in one shade of brown or another, from near black to dull yellow. One corner was all bookshelves full of matched sets so big and thick they could only be read on a table. He sank into an easy chair in the corner and waved me to the couch on his right. He talked like he'd written it all out and memorized it. His voice was husky enough to make me think he overused it regularly and he stared at me like I was a delinquent and he was the school principal.

"I decided to drop assault charges against you," he announced, "not because Officer Schoop insisted they wouldn't stand up in court, but because my son admitted he struck first. I strongly suspect you goaded him into it but since Rex is opposed to me making charges I've decided to honor his wishes."

He waited for a sign of gratitude. I blinked, owl style.

He decided I didn't have the social grace for polite chitchat and started toward his point.

"I understand you're painting street signs for the town. How long will that take?"

"Week and a half."

"Working eight hours a day?"

"Now and again I take a break."

"How'd you like to make some extra money?"

"That'd depend."

"On what, besides the pay?"

"What I was getting paid for."

He smiled thinly. "Good. You're particular. What I have in mind is a housepainting job on a place I own on the north side. You could work three hours an evening and probably get the job done in less than a week."

"What's it pay?"

"Dollar an hour."

"No, thanks."

"I could hire a local for half that."

"So hire him."

"You consider housepainting beneath you, is that it?"

"I'm not interested in eleven-hour working days."

"And besides, you have other things to do evenings, right?"

"I usually manage."

He was silent for a moment and I pulled out my makings and started building a cigarette. He got up, went to a table, pulled a cigar box from a drawer, and offered me one. They were panatelas. I put my bag and paper away and took one. He helped himself, took a lighter from the tabletop, and fired us both up.

"Care for a sherry?" he asked.

"Brandy'd be better."

He raised an eyebrow, went to a cabinet, and returned with a brandy bottle on a tray and two glasses. The bottle had a profile of Napoleon. The brandy was dark and rich.

After we'd both tried the stuff and puffed our turns he managed another thin smile.

"What has Sullivan offered you to solve the Genevieve killing?" he asked.

"Nothing. When he hired me to do the signs he told me don't rile prominent citizens like Mr. Tobler. How come he worries about your peace of mind?"

He blew smoke in a small ring and shook his head.

"Mayor Sullivan is a smart politician. Cagey, even. We've been on opposite sides all our lives but this is a small town and we have to live with each other. So we're careful about how and when we make a move that'll stir up trouble. He knows I don't want all that old gossip and nonsense dredged up again. The poor girl was obviously killed by a thwarted lover; no one was able to discover who four years ago and it's less than likely anyone, particularly an outsider, is going to dig up the solution at this late date. My son was everybody's favorite for the villain because he's better looking than most and had been her steadiest boyfriend. But sworn testimony gave him an absolute alibi and I know damned well he didn't do the murder. Officer Schoop has something like a guilt complex about the Genevieve case that's more than abnormal. It's a sick obsession, which is enough to make a reasonable man wonder what his involvement might've been with a girl young enough to be his daughter. However, Schoop's very popular with the locals so when he wanted you to have a job, Sullivan went along, knowing what he had in mind. But our mayor's too smart to want you really doing anything. So far, all you've managed is a brawl with my son and the loss of your shelter. The offer I've made would keep you busy and out of trouble—and the pay isn't contemptible."

"What sort of trouble you think'll come next?" I asked.

He let loose a couple more smoke rings. They were tight and rolled like alive.

"I've no crystal ball or psychic powers. But it doesn't take a wizard to guess there'll be more than you can handle."

The cigar and brandy suddenly seemed too much. I butted out the cigar only a third smoked, moved the brandy glass an inch toward Tobler, and stood up.

"Well, thanks for everything, including the forecast. I'll probably see you around."

"You're making a mistake," he said, smiling as he got to his feet.

"Story of my life. But while I'm at it—how'd you get on with Genevieve? I hear she worked here now and again. Ever get acquainted?"

"My wife works with the help, I had little exposure."

"So it didn't matter if she was alive or dead?"

"Careful, Mr. Wilcox. Remember what the mayor told you."

I said I'd give it a try and left.

6

TUESDAY THE WIND was up and the dust with it. I had to keep the windows closed but made out because the mayor finally sent over the promised fan and besides, dust clouded the sun and dropped the heat a little.

McGinty, who delivered the fan, hung around watching me letter signs.

"Hear you went to see Tobler last night," he said.

"Where'd that come from?"

"Neighbor saw him let you in. Said you were there near an hour."

"She tell you what we talked about?"

He cackled. "Nope. I'm supposed to find out."

"Tell the neighbor he wanted me to paint a house he owns over on the north side."

"After you do this job?"

"He figured I'd do it evenings."

He was quiet a moment and I didn't look his way. Finally he said, "That'll give you a pretty full day, huh?"

"It would if I'd taken it."

More silence. Then, "It didn't take no hour to cover that."

"It wasn't any hour. We had cigars and a little drink, which didn't take more than half an hour."

He seemed to think that was pretty funny. I asked why.

He said the picture of me sitting in Tobler's living room, smoking one of his skinny cigars and swigging his fancy booze, was pretty hard for him to frame.

I admitted it did call for some imagination.

"He get on you any for the fracas with Rex?"

"He said he wasn't going to sue me."

"So you parted pals, huh?"

"Not quite."

He wandered off after that but showed up when I was having lunch at Mirabelle's Do Drop Inn and sat beside me at the counter.

I asked if he knew the teacher, Galbraith. He said sure, did I want to talk with him? I nodded and he swung around on the stool and waved at a booth near the front window.

"That's him alone there. The floppy-haired guy."

I thanked him, took my cup of coffee, moved over to the booth, and introduced myself. He had a book open before him and at first stared at me like a man in a trance, then blinked and smiled. It showed white teeth, deep dimples, bright blue eyes, and almost unnatural warmth.

"I've heard of you," he said. "Sit down."

"Don't believe all you hear," I said, accepting the invitation.

"In Greenhill, that's a given."

"The book must be a good one."

He glanced down, smiling. "Yes, I was rather absorbed, even though I've read it before. It's Norman Douglas's *Southwind*. A fantastic work. Not one I could very handily offer in my English classes."

"Why not?"

"Well, it's rather subtle, for one thing, but I suppose the greater problem is that a staid English bishop ends up condoning a murder."

"You go along with the bishop?"

"Oh yes, in the context of this novel. I suppose that interests you, since you've been involved in murders a few times."

"Yeah, and like the bishop, I even thought a couple of them were called for. You mind talking about one of your old students?"

"You mean Genevieve, of course. What can I tell you?"

"What kind of a girl was she?"

He glanced at the page number of his book, closed it, and leaned into the wall corner of the booth.

"She was a bright, lovely woman-child. Not as brilliant as many said after she was gone, not even as beautiful, I'm afraid. But well above average. She had a charming eagerness, great energy, and, I suspect, rather high ambitions."

"Like what?"

"To make the most of herself, live to the utmost, and make everyone love her."

"Did you?"

"Some, yes. I don't think anyone could resist."

"You married?"

"Oh yes. My wife's in a TB sanatorium, so at the present I live like a bachelor without one's freedom."

"Were you married when Genevieve was your student?"

"No. The year after. Less a month or so. When I said I loved Genevieve some, it wasn't in a carnal or even a romantic sense. She was just a very lovable girl but I would never have tried to make anything of it. In the first place she was almost constantly surrounded by friends so even if I'd had sneaky hopes, it would've been impossible to promote them and I'm sure you know, it would be a disaster for a schoolteacher in this town to stir even the faintest of rumors about interest in a student beyond the classroom."

That speech made me believe he'd wanted the worst way to make out but hadn't had the balls or inventiveness to manage it. And I also considered that was exactly what he wanted me to think.

He gave me a rueful grin. "Do I protest too much?"

I waved that off and asked if he had any notion who might have planted the baby.

"No. But certainly I thought of it enough. I can't really believe it was any of the students. I told you, Genevieve was an ambitious girl, and I'm afraid, pretty calculating, even manipulative."

"You think old man Tobler could've got in?"

He studied me a little before answering, "It's hard to imagine how. Every working day he's at his Ford agency and while his wife does a great deal of gadding about day and night, he's usually with her for the night activities. I don't say that, implying that he'd do something given the chance."

"You know Mrs. Tobler?"

"Marvel? Oh sure. You can't be in this town long and not know her."

"What's she like?"

"She's five by five, with short black hair and wonderful eyes. Exceptionally intelligent, witty, and clever. It may sound ridiculous when I've called her five by five, but she's actually sexy in spite of that. The only woman I've ever met who can make a man feel like a man and at the same time always let him know she's smarter than he is."

"Where could I meet her without going to her house?"

"At the library. She pretty much runs it. Spends a lot of time there."

"When's it open?"

"Wednesday nights and Saturday from ten till five."

I thanked him and went back to the hall and my sign painting.

At suppertime I found McGinty in a booth at Mirabelle's and he waved me over the moment I stepped in the café.

"Jim Baltz is home," he told me. "Old man had a stroke and Jim got leave to come take over till he can find somebody to keep the place going."

"What's his job in Aberdeen?"

"He's at the Normal School there. That's like where they teach teachers to teach."

"In summer?"

"No. In summer he works in a grocery store, I think."

"Where's the farm?"

"Just off County Five, about three miles west of town. You gonna go see him?"

I said I might. He offered to show me the way. I agreed.

The wind was easing off as the sun headed west, shining in my eyes till I squinted hard enough to wrinkle my skull. It was a relief when we turned north on the drive up to the farmhouse built on a slope facing south. Beyond the two-story white house a windbreak of elms ran east and west. They'd been planted too close together and looked scruffy.

A young man shoved the screen door open at a side door and stepped down from the stoop to greet us. McGinty asked him how his father was doing.

"Fair," said the young man, studying me.

"This here's Carl Wilcox," said McGinty. "You maybe heard about him. He's painting street signs for Greenhill."

Jim Baltz gave no indication he had or hadn't heard of me. His light brown hair hadn't been trimmed in a while but his shave was close enough to make his cheeks shine and the freckles stand out bright. He shook hands with a firm grip and suggested we come inside for a cup.

We moved into a big, high-ceilinged kitchen with the usual high cabinets, the cistern pump at the sink, and a white-topped table in the center. There were only two chairs and Jim hustled off to fetch a couple more while his mother stood by the range examining McGinty and me. She was a stocky woman with dark, gray-streaked hair, chubby cheeks, a thin mouth, and dimpled chin.

I said hi, I'm Carl, and she said she was Signe, Jim's mother.

"Signe," McGinty told me, "makes the best strawberry-rhubarb pie in the county."

"Sweet talk'll get you nothing," she told him. "I haven't baked since Pa had his stroke."

Jim returned with chairs and the conversation stayed mostly on the old man upstairs. They told us he was partially paralyzed but starting to recover his mind, which had been muzzy a day or two.

Finally we got around to Genevieve, and Jim's impressions of her were straight dream memories. According to him, she was a beautiful, angelic girl of exceptional intelligence and absolute purity.

I asked if he had any idea who had killed her and he looked at me for several seconds before saying he didn't think it would be right for him to say.

"Why?" I asked.

"You'd think I was just jealous and vindictive."

"So you figure it was Rex," said McGinty.

He sighed and said, "Well, yes, I'm afraid so."

"What about the alibi he got from Dutro?" I asked.

He got a pained look, glanced at his mother, and finally said, "Dewey lied, flat out."

"How'd you know that?"

"Because he told me so."

7

"DUTRO LIVES IN Aberdeen?" I asked.

"That's right. We see each other almost every weekend."

"How come he admitted to you the alibi was a lie?"

"It just happens we both know a certain girl in Aberdeen. She admitted to me a while back that the night Dewey said he and Rex were boozing together, he was actually with her and they didn't have company. When I put that to Dewey, he admitted she told me the truth."

"Why'd he lie to the cops?"

"He said it was because he and Rex were old pals and Rex needed the alibi and swore he hadn't been near Genevieve that night."

"Tell him about Al Tobler's little loan," said his mother.

Jim scowled. "Dewey got a student loan from Al Tobler right after Gen was killed. Maybe it was just a coincidence."

I stared at him and he squirmed uncomfortably.

"I suppose," he said, "you're wondering why I'm telling you this."

"Uh-huh."

He glanced at his mother. "We talked about it last night and

I got remembering what a bastard Rex could be back when we were both after Gen. You see, after she died, all of us who'd been crazy about her were practically like a club and we felt so damn bad we just couldn't believe any of us would've done it. That's why I figured at first Rex hadn't killed her but needed an alibi if he wasn't going to get nailed, so Dewey's story was like a white lie. But last night, the more we went over it the more I started thinking it had to be Rex because he's the only one of us that'd do such a thing. He was always losing his temper and going wild."

"You ever go all the way with Gen?" I asked.

"No. It's hard to believe anybody ever did—she went nuts if you tried to go too far. I mean, she wasn't big at all but she could really fight and she didn't care what she did to you."

"She ever talk about the Tobler family?"

"Not a bit. She just acted as if she were family—not a girl working for the rich neighbor."

"You get any notion what she thought of Al?"

"She didn't talk about him. The only time she mentioned his name she called him Mr. Tobler."

I looked at Signe.

"You ever hear stories about Al Tobler?"

"What kind of stories?"

"Is he interested in women besides his wife?"

"All men are interested in other women. That's a stupid question."

"They don't all get talked about."

"People are careful about talking against a man like Tobler."

"So, did anybody talk carefully about him that you heard?"

She said no they didn't talk about him any way, and poured her cool coffee remains into the sink.

I asked Jim if he'd give the name of the girl in Aberdeen who shot Rex's alibi. He said it wouldn't do me any good, she'd run off to California with a married pharmacist and nobody knew where they lived because of course the druggist didn't want his wife to catch up with him.

I said I'd still like to have the name.

"It was Lorraine Knight," said Signe.

Her son gave her a look that fell some short of fond.

On the drive back to town I asked McGinty what he thought of our visit.

"Signe put him up to telling you about the bum alibi."

"Yeah. You think he lied about the girl running off with a druggist?"

McGinty shook his head. "I remember the story. A druggist named Terry Bock ran off with Lorraine. You know what the guys called her? Doozy. They said she was free to friends and didn't have an enemy in the world. Old Bock fell like a ton of bricks and just carried her off."

It was near dark when we got back to town and split up. Officer Schoop wasn't in his office at City Hall when I dropped around. I glanced in the window of the soda fountain while heading for the hotel and saw the Coverly sisters at a table just inside. Steffi waved at me eagerly so I went in and joined them.

"I've figured out why you're a traveling sign painter," said Steffi. "It's just an excuse to hang around towns and solve murders."

"You got a great imagination."

"Oh no. It's exciting, isn't it? Everybody's talking about you and thinking about what happened all over again and taking sides."

"It's not all that humming," said Holly, but she grinned at me in a new way. "What you are is sort of a Pied Piper in reverse. Instead of coming into town and piping away the troubles, you bring them all out into the open."

"How come," I said, "since Saturday night I haven't seen Rex Tobler?"

"He went back to Aberdeen," said Holly. "He works on a used car lot, which makes his father very unhappy because he wanted him working here in Greenhill, so he could take over the family business one day."

I thought that was very interesting.

"Maybe he's not in Aberdeen at all," said Steffi. "I bet he skipped to England or someplace."

I asked if they had heard the story about Doozy Knight and the fellow from the drugstore in Aberdeen.

"Sure," said Holly, "that was just last year. Jim Baltz told me about it."

"He tell you anything else about her?"

"Like what?"

"Like she'd told him the alibi Dewey Dutro gave Rex was a phony."

Her eyes went wide and her mouth made a small O.

"You're kidding."

"No."

"My God." She stared at her half glass of Coke a moment, then her mouth twisted and she looked at her sister.

"And you let him kiss you, huh?" said Steffi.

"I can't believe it," said Holly but it was plain she did.

"That he killed Gen or you let him kiss you?" demanded the little sister.

"Either—I don't know." She looked at me. "I'm glad you knocked him down. I wish you'd killed him."

"Sure, that'd been neat," said Steffi. She was very good with sarcasm.

"Oh shut up," said Holly. She pushed her chair back and stood a second, staring at the table, then at me.

"Let's go for a walk."

I said okay and got up. The little sister poked the ice cream at the bottom of her soda and looked sullen.

Outside was quiet, the air sweet and still warm from the

day's hard sun. We walked west slowly past the closed shops. The streetlights were on, attracting the evening bugs. A car came from the east, slowed through town, and increased speed once more half a block beyond us.

"I suppose it had to be Rex," she said. "I think we all accepted the alibi because we just didn't want anybody we knew to be bad enough to kill Genevieve. He's not really all bad, you know. Just moody and temperamental. What makes it so hard to believe is, I'm positive if he made her pregnant he'd have been glad to marry her. He's awfully jealous and possessive and there just wasn't anybody else he gave a darn for in those days. There was some talk he had girls in Aberdeen, but that was because Gen wouldn't let him go as far as he wanted to with her and he hoped to make her jealous."

"Did you think she was a virgin?" I asked.

"I assumed it. The truth is, while we saw a lot of each other, we weren't confiding pals. Genevieve wasn't really comfortable with anyone she considered competition—and she always thought of me that way. I was never as popular, but she heard too often I was the prettiest girl in Greenhill and she didn't exactly love that."

We wound up back at her house. I half expected to find Steffi waiting on the porch but the swing was deserted and we parked on it.

"How come you've never married?" she asked.

"I did, once."

"What happened?"

"She went back east—it didn't work out."

"Did she get pregnant before or after you got married?"

"Before."

"Is that why you married her?"

"It was one of the reasons."

"What happened to the baby?"

"She aborted it."

She sensed my discomfort with the conversation and was still for a few seconds but couldn't hold out.

"Is that why you split up?"

"It was one of the reasons."

"You didn't want her to, huh?"

"She never asked. Just did it."

That brought some more silence. Someone came out the front door of the house to our left and walked toward Main Street. She didn't speak again until the person's back was receding.

"Did you think she trapped you into marrying her and then got rid of the baby?"

"No. She was afraid of pain. And she didn't think she'd be any good with a kid."

She reached over and patted my hand.

"I think you've been hurt badly," she said.

I couldn't think of a snappy answer for that one and when I faced her she leaned my way until I kissed her nice and easy.

Her mouth was soft and warm. Before I could make more of it she drew back carefully with her hands on my chest.

"Have you ever made any other girl pregnant?" she asked.

"That's hard to answer," I had to admit.

"Because you love them and leave them, right?"

"It's happened."

"What would you do if you knew you got a girl pregnant?"

"It'd depend, I guess."

"On what?"

"How I felt about her."

She laughed and stood up.

"I've asked that question lots of times," she said. "I think you're the only one who's ever been even close to honest. Most of them get terribly embarrassed or very earnest."

"What'd Rex answer?"

"He got earnest. He said he would very definitely marry me."

"Did you ask him what he'd do if he got Genevieve pregnant?"

"No. I wasn't smart enough to pin him on that."

"Did he have reason to think he'd made you pregnant?"

"No. I may not be brilliant but I'm not that dumb. Good night, Carl."

I didn't get another kiss.

8

AFTER DINNER WEDNESDAY evening I ambled over
to the Greenhill Library. It was in a house almost big enough
to call a mansion just a block off Main Street and kitty-corner
from the Lutheran Church. The entrance was a side door
approached by a walk around the right. I went through a
small vestibule where people parked coats and overshoes in
the winter and on into a large room with shelves along all
four walls. In its center a large oak table bellied up to a wide
desk where Mrs. Tobler sat facing the door. The teacher,
Galbraith, had described her well. She was fat, but her smooth
face had fine features, beautiful teeth, and bright dark eyes
that met mine directly the moment I stepped in the room. The
black, glossy hair was trimmed short and brushed to square her
face a little.

"Well," she said, "Mr. Carl Wilcox, I presume."

I said "Mrs. Tobler" and nodded.

"What kind of book are you looking for?" she asked.

"You got *Martin Eden*?"

"As a matter of fact, we do, but I'd have expected you to ask
for *The Call of the Wild*."

"I've read it," I said, pulling out a chair by the table to sit down.

"What else have you read?"

"*Smokey* and a couple others by Will James."

"Oh yes. A cowboy, wasn't he?"

"Yeah. He also served time."

"Something in common with you. Any other cowboy works?"

"I liked *Happy Hawkins.*"

"I'm afraid I don't know that one—who wrote it?"

"Robert Alexander Wason."

"Oh. Doesn't ring a bell."

"What'd you think of Genevieve?" I asked.

"Is that the name of a book?"

"No. It's a girl who worked for you."

"Ah, Genny Sinclair. So it isn't books you're really after."

"A little learning," I said.

"This is the right place for that. I liked Genny. I could almost say I loved her. But not quite."

"Why not quite?"

"A good question. One I asked myself many times after her death. Why wasn't I more damaged by her dying, especially considering the manner of it? I'm not sure. Maybe I was a little jealous—she made too much of an impression on my son and husband. She was too young, slim and pretty, too full of energy, charm, and ambition. All the time she was with us I kept wondering exactly what she was after and gradually it dawned on me, she wanted everything. My boy, my husband, my house, my world. She had an insatiable hunger. Nobody else realized that, but it was there so naked and plain in everything she did, from the way she dressed and talked to her way of becoming indispensable. I suppose this is beginning to sound as if I hated her, but I never did. I'll admit she worried and upset me at times. The most tiresome part was seeing her so clearly when no one else did. It was enough to make me feel paranoid."

"You know Holly?"

"The Coverly girl? Of course. She and Genevieve seemed close, although I suspect Genny always hated the fact Holly was better looking."

"That's what Holly thought."

"Isn't that interesting? But I'm not too surprised. Holly always struck me as very quick. I never could understand why Genny was more popular with boys but I suppose Holly intimidated them. Too smart and good looking."

"If Gen bothered you that much, how come you kept her on?"

"There was no graceful way to handle it. I couldn't claim she was incompetent, lazy, or careless. She simply never was. How do you tell two infatuated men in your family that you can't bear the competition? Besides that—as I said in the beginning—I couldn't help liking her myself. I couldn't find any way to get rid of her without losing my self-respect."

"So who do you think could have?"

"I can only guess it was one of the men she led on but didn't give in to. There were so many of them. . . ."

"Who that you know?"

"You mean besides my boy and husband? Well, there's the Irishman Mutt O'Keefe, Jim Baltz, and that schoolteacher Galbraith for starters. I suspect there were others who panted for her."

"Your boy, Rex, claims an alibi. Does your husband have one?"

"Why, me, of course."

"He was home that night?"

"Yes."

"So you both have an alibi."

She smiled prettily. "That's right. Does that strike you as a bit too convenient?"

I got up and wandered over to the bookshelves. They had a

big collection of Tom Swift books I remembered my nephew had liked. I couldn't get into them.

"What's your next step, Mr. Wilcox?" she asked.

"I'm thinking of a run to Aberdeen," I said, turning back to her.

"To check out Rex's alibi?"

"Uh-huh."

"That's a waste of time. There's no reason on earth Rex would kill Genevieve. He loved her."

"That's one of the oldest reasons for killing," I said.

She looked down at the desk. I could see the dark hair was quite thin and guessed it was dyed. She looked up.

"I suppose you're wondering why I was so open about my feelings toward Genny."

"It made me wonder."

"My husband thinks you're a dangerous man. He said I shouldn't talk with you at all. I told him I'd not only talk to you, I'd tell everything straight."

"What'd he say to that?"

"He said maybe I was smarter than he was."

"I guess that wasn't a new discovery."

She laughed. "Al's a lot of things, vain, overambitious, thin-skinned, and sometimes a tough son of a bitch. But don't underestimate him. Dumb he's not."

"He's smart enough to know who's really with it, though."

"And I'm smart enough to spot a snow job."

I leaned against the table, grinning at her. She grinned back.

"You drive the family car?"

"Sure. Probably more than Al does."

"And so does Rex, right?"

"That's right. But not that night. The car stayed in the garage all evening. Rex never had keys of his own."

"How long you had the car you got?"

"Only a year—so it won't do any good checking it out for blood or dents."

"It wouldn't be much use even if you'd had it four years. Al says she was just run over, not into. There wasn't much blood around except what was loose inside her where broken ribs poked holes through her veins and arteries."

Her smile disappeared. "All right," she said, "you take this thing seriously. So do I. Don't try to rub my nose in the mess. I like to treat it from a distance because it's too hard to handle any other way. I'd help you if I could. I can't. So leave me alone."

I thanked her and left.

9

IN THE MORNING I told Mayor Sullivan my plan to visit Aberdeen. He didn't like it until he heard what Jim Baltz had said about Rex's alibi. Then his chubby face lit up like a politician discovering his opponent may be in the soup.

"Well, some progress! All right. Talk with Dutro but avoid Rex Tobler. You'd just get in a brawl and the police there wouldn't be as tolerant as Al. I think Mac should go with you. He knows the town fairly well, has friends there."

"McGinty?"

"Yes."

"Why?"

"You want a witness along, and just now it'd be smart to avoid being alone any more than you can help."

"Mr. Mayor, I got a little problem picturing McGinty as a bodyguard."

"That's not the idea. The fact is, him being around would make it much harder for anyone wanting to get rid of you. Your companion doesn't need to be a bully with a gun, just someone known locally and well accepted."

I shrugged and an hour later McGinty and I were on the road

heading north to Aberdeen. Sullivan's notions didn't convince me I needed McGinty but the old man had his own ideas.

"Don't know whether I'm a baby-sitter or a deputy," he said.

"You're neither," I told him. "Your job is just to be in the way if Al Tobler or his friends try to nix me."

"What'd keep 'em from nixing me too?"

"Sullivan figures they'd think that was getting too messy. And besides, you're a native and lovable."

"That's true. A man old as I am but still frisky, can make the younguns feel comfortable if he's not too pushy. You know how you can tell when you're really getting old?"

"Not yet."

"It's when you get varicose veins in your dong. That's when."

"Well, at least it doesn't show often, huh?"

"It's a good reason for screwing in the dark. And the only ones I can still get look best then too. You getting anywhere with Holly?"

"Haven't tried."

He gave me a wise look and was still for a while before asking what my plans were in Aberdeen.

I said we'd look up Dutro and maybe nose around to see if I could find Rex.

Once in town we located a telephone book, found Dutro's address, and I gave him a call. There was no answer, which didn't surprise me any—I figured he was probably at work and asked McGinty where that'd be.

"Last I heard he was working for a men's clothing store, Brattman's I think."

I looked up the address, drove over, and found a dapper old dude in a double-breasted pinstripe suit straightening up a table of shirts. He frowned at first sight of us but then dredged up a smile and walked our way. I guess he'd been in the business too long to let his first impressions dampen his natural salesman's optimism. The smile revealed fine store teeth and he spoke as friendly as if he believed we might be looking for new suits.

"Is Dutro around?" I asked.

"No, but I can help. I'm the owner here."

"Wanted to talk with him about a friend of his. Where could we find him?"

"He lives on South Third Street. You'll find the number in the telephone book."

"Tried that. No answer."

"So did I." His tone was sour.

"He miss work before?"

"A couple times. Usually on Mondays, though. He's a good salesman so I've let it pass. Why do you want him?"

"He ever mention anything to you about a murder in his hometown a few years back?"

He lost his smile and became wary. "Are you a cop?"

"I'm doing some checking for Mayor Sullivan in Greenhill. Dutro gave an alibi for one of the suspects and we'd like to check it out a little."

"Dewey's not a suspect?"

"No."

"I'm relieved. But I'll admit it bothers me I couldn't reach him this morning when I called. The other times he missed work I got him right away and he was terribly apologetic."

I questioned him until I was sure he had nothing for us and went back to the car with McGinty in tow.

"Now what?" asked McGinty.

"We'll go knock," I said.

Dutro lived on the second floor of a duplex. I knocked several times on the lower door after trying the bell, which made no sound I could hear. After the third pounding the lower-level door opened and soft-faced woman wearing a head scarf peered at us and said she didn't think Mr. Dutro was in and would I kindly knock off trying to beat the door down.

"Do you know if he's been around today?" I asked.

"I haven't heard him so I guess not. Didn't hear him come in last night and I usually do."

No, she said in answer to my question, she wasn't well acquainted with Dewey. He was friendly, quiet, and paid his rent regular and that was the extent of it. I explained he hadn't reported to work and that brought a worried look. It didn't take much more talk to persuade her she should check up. She asked us to wait in the hall and went up, unlocked the door, and entered. A few seconds later she was back.

"He's not there and the bed's made."

She didn't know if he had any family although she had noticed he got mail now and then from Greenhill.

She was willing for me to use her phone for a collect call to Greenhill and I got Sullivan after a short delay. He said he'd check with Dutro's parents, who were still living in town, and get back to me.

The lady offered us coffee while we waited for the call back and then excused herself. I answered when the phone rang and it was Sullivan. He said the parents hadn't heard from Dutro during the past week and had no idea why he wasn't at work. They said he'd been going with a young woman named Myra Payne. They thought she lived with her parents but didn't know the father's name.

Between my first call and the call back the duplex lady returned with the kerchief removed and her hair brushed out. She'd also switched from a robe and slippers to a blue housedress with buttons down the front. It looked so nice I wished I'd left McGinty in Greenhill. She said her name was Dotty Drexell and she was a widow.

"I bet it hasn't been for long," I said.

"Not long enough to get used to," she admitted and offered coffee.

While we drank it I learned Rex Tobler had visited Dewey at least once. She didn't know the name but her description fit.

She thought they'd been together Tuesday night.

On the second call to Paynes listed in the directory I found Myra. When I explained why I was calling she hung up.

I called Sullivan again and eventually he said he'd call the police and I should go around and talk with them.

So I did.

10

OFFICER DAHLBERG OUTWEIGHED me by a good
one hundred pounds and had a clear top view of my noggin since
his eyes took in the world from six inches above mine. He'd
talked personally with Mayor Sullivan, who had filled him in on
all important details. It made him friendly as a spaniel pup and
he didn't worry about why the mayor of Greenhill had a bum
like me running official errands. He was one of those men,
beloved by all in authority, who never ask awkward questions
when a superior gives him an assignment. After talking things
over at the police station we drove back to Dutro's place in his
cop car and searched the room under the landlady's disapproving eyes. She wasn't pleased when Dahlberg pulled the made-up
bed apart checking for hidden items, but when he awkwardly
tried to pull it straight again she shooed him off and did it herself
while we went through the closet.

We didn't find anything but ordinary clothes, a small stack of
Liberty and *Collier's* magazines, and one copy of *Spicy Detective* at
the bottom of the *Liberty* pile. There were no letters around, and no
address book. Dahlberg found a telephone number written on the
cover of the telephone directory and I recognized it as Myra Payne's.

When I told Officer Dahlberg about her he grunted, looked up the address, and said we'd wheel around and get acquainted.

I suggested that McGinty wait in the car so the lady wouldn't feel ganged up on. Mac didn't like that but Dahlberg approved and we went up to the door and he hit the bell button.

The inside door opened cautiously and a small brown-haired woman peered at us with distrustful eyes.

"Myra Payne?" asked Dahlberg.

"I'm her mother. What do you want?"

"Like to talk to her a bit. I'm Officer Dahlberg, this is Mr. Wilcox from Greenhill. Your daughter's home, isn't she?"

The mother confessed to that and when Dahlberg suggested she invite us in she pushed the screen and we stepped back and then inside, following her into a hall with a stairway to the right and a living room on the left. She waved us into the latter and said she'd get her daughter and started up the stairs.

It was a small neatly kept room with the usual couch and matching easy chair in brown, a huge woven rag rug, and a pair of wooden chairs with upholstered seats and padded arms. There were dark drapes on the windows, all drawn just short of closed so the burning sun shafted through, making motes shine in the still air.

We sat in the padded wooden chairs and Dahlberg grinned at me as we heard angry voices upstairs.

"I think the girl's got a problem explaining why cops are at the door," he said.

The voices, which had flared like a radio turned on too loud, went silent. A few moments later we heard steps coming down the stairs.

Myra and her mother looked almost like sisters. Their hair was dark brown and carefully curled, they had slightly snubbed noses, round chins, and large blue eyes. Myra's forehead wasn't quite as high as her mother's and her mouth was smaller. Now the lips were tight with anger and maybe fear. She only glanced at Dahlberg but gave me a hard stare.

"What's he told you?" she asked Dahlberg, still glaring at me.

"He told me Mr. Dutro didn't show up for work today and wasn't home when he went there trying to locate him. His landlady doesn't think he came home last night. When Wilcox tried to call you for help you hung up on him. I've been to Mr. Dutro's place and he's definitely not there and we are concerned. Aren't you?"

"Dewey's all right. We had dinner last night and he told me all about this man and what's going on in Greenhill where they're trying to prove Rex Tobler killed that girl years ago. He said they're trying to call him a liar because he gave Rex an alibi and he's afraid of what's going on and he's going to California for a while until this all quiets down."

"Where in California?"

"I don't know and wouldn't tell you if I did."

"Myra!" exclaimed her mother.

Myra, ignoring her, continued glaring at me defiantly. Then she switched to Dahlberg.

"Do you know this man already attacked and beat up on Rex Tobler at a dance hall in Greenhill?"

"That's not quite the story we got," said Dahlberg. "The way we hear it, Tobler started the fight, which only lasted a couple seconds before the Greenhill cop stopped it. This cop saw the whole thing so you can't make a case for Wilcox beating up on anybody. On top of that there was a whole crowd witnessed the fracas and nobody tells it different."

"That's because they're all down on Rex because he was foolish enough to run around with that little hussy who got herself killed."

Dahlberg nodded calmly. "I can see Mr. Dutro has given you quite a story. But I'm afraid it won't hold water if he's run off. Are you positive he's gone on the run?"

She lowered her eyes a moment and twisted her hands in

her lap. When she looked up her mouth softened and she suddenly looked pretty and worried.

"No. I just said that. He only told me he was thinking about it. He was awfully afraid."

"What'd he tell you he was afraid of?" I asked.

She glanced at me, still hostile but not quite so intense about it.

"He was afraid of you. Rex told him you'd come after him and would be around to make him say he hadn't really been with Rex that night."

"Did he tell you he'd given Tobler a phony alibi?"

"No." She looked at her hands again.

"How long've you known him?" I asked.

"We met at Aberdeen Normal our senior year. Graduated together. He's going to teach in North Dakota, at Fargo starting this fall."

"Were you engaged?"

"No. We talked about it some but decided to wait a year."

"Did he ever tell you about a girl named Lorraine Knight?"

She shook her head.

"She's a girl he was actually with that night," I said.

"I don't believe that," she flared.

"Do you know Jim Baltz?"

"I never met him. Dewey mentioned the name a couple times. He's the farmer's son, isn't he?"

"Uh-huh. Did you know Al Tobler paid Dewey's tuition through college?"

She glanced at Dahlberg, then back at me. "Are you saying he was bribed for that alibi?"

"The timing was pretty good."

"It wasn't a gift. It was a loan."

"So Dewey's paying him back?"

"He will when he starts teaching. He hasn't made enough money selling clothes to more than cover his keep. That's one of the reasons he didn't want us to get married quite yet. He wanted to be free of debt."

We talked some more but got no help in figuring out where Dewey might be. He had a brother in California, which is why she mentioned the idea of his going there. She admitted he had promised to write. She finally agreed she'd try to persuade him to talk with us if she found out where he was.

Dahlberg felt sure she would follow through. I wasn't. Not because she'd hold out but because I didn't think she'd hear.

11

I'D EXPECTED TO find Rex through Dutro and with the man missing, the trip seemed at a dead end. Dahlberg okayed my making a couple calls to Greenhill and I tried Holly first. Steffi answered and told me her sister was downtown. I explained my problem and she was sympathetic but not helpful.

"Holly probably couldn't tell you anything either. Actually, she only went out with Rex a couple times—she never liked him much and only went out with him because she thought he was treated bad by some of the people that were nuts about Gen. She thought they sort of made him a goat."

After that I called Marvel Tobler and told her Dutro had disappeared and we needed any help we could get to locate him. Could she give me her son's address in Aberdeen so we could check with him?

"Really, Mr. Wilcox, aren't you being rather transparent? The truth is you simply want to talk with my son, isn't that it?"

"I'd figured on it. But Dewey didn't show up for work and according to his landlady, didn't come home last night. I'm calling from the Aberdeen police station—they've searched Dewey's apartment for some lead on why he's gone or where and came up with nothing. We've talked with his girlfriend, Myra Payne, who had dinner with him last night. She says he told her he was scared of me and was thinking of ducking out of town, but didn't tell her where or when he'd go."

There was a long silence on the line.

"Mrs. Tobler?" I asked.

"I'm still here," she said. "Trying to think."

"Was Rex going to stay with him?"

I heard her draw a deep breath and finally she said, "No."

"How about some girlfriend?"

"I don't know. Rex hasn't confided all that much in his mama lately."

"How about your husband? Would he know if Rex was planning a trip somewhere besides Aberdeen?"

"Rex talks less with his father than he does with me."

She was silent for another few seconds and finally asked how she could know I was calling from the police department.

"Hang up and call back. Ask the operator for police."

"All right, I'm going to do that."

Dahlberg was on the line with her a few moments later and she told him to check with her sister, Beulah Kruger. She was a widow living on a farm south of Aberdeen with in-laws named Simpson.

She gave directions and half an hour later Dahlberg and I were approaching the farm. McGinty had stayed in Aberdeen, having decided to spend some time in the hardware store for a visit with an old friend.

The woman who came to the door as we approached the house was tall and slim as a whippet so I assumed she was Mrs. Simpson. When Dahlberg asked she informed him she was Mrs. Kruger.

"Fine," said Dahlberg, handing her his friendly smile. "We'd like to see your nephew, Rex. Understand he's staying here."

She looked at him a second, then at me, and back to him. Her brown eyes had flecks of gold and the lashes were long enough to look heavy. Her gaze would make a man with imagination nervous.

"Why?"

The look didn't bother Dahlberg any. "It's a little complicated—mind if we come in and talk?"

Beulah Kruger was so different from her sister I was convinced they'd not shared the same father. She looked over Dahlberg's uniform, gave me another suspicious look, and let us in. We sat in the parlor, which was larger than most you find on a farm. In fact, the whole house was larger than average.

"Where's Rex?" Dahlberg asked.

"Hunting gophers," she said.

"Was he here last night?"

"Why're you asking?"

Dahlberg gave her his comforting smile and said this here was just a routine checkup. We were trying to find a missing man who was a friend of Rex's and needed some help.

"Who?"

"Dewey Dutro. You know him?"

"I've heard of him," she said. "I know from your uniform you're a cop, but who's this?"

Dahlberg looked at me.

"His name's Carl Wilcox. He's been asked by the mayor of Greenhill to help out on a case we got."

"He's the one beat up on Rex last Saturday night."

"Is that what Rex told you?"

"That's right."

"He tell you it happened in a dance hall in front of the town cop and a dozen witnesses that said Rex started it?"

Beulah's dark eyes had been glaring at me but that made her transfer it to him.

"No. Were you there?"

"Nope. Whatever happened there, no one's pressed any charges and that's not what this visit's about. When you expect Rex back?"

"When I see him. That could be in ten minutes, might be in as many days. He's free and can do as he darned well pleases."

"Where does he hunt gophers?" Dahlberg asked.

"In the fields, where'd you think?"

"Any particular ones?"

"No, any gopher will do."

"I meant particular fields."

"I've no idea."

"Was he around here last night?"

"Yes."

"For dinner and on?"

"That's right."

Her mouth was wide and hostility gave it a mean look. I figured if she smiled it'd be a dandy. Her feistiness tickled me.

Dahlberg stalled around, trying to think of some sharp questions, but finally gave up and we went outside.

"I shouldn't have brought you along," he complained.

"You're right."

We got in the car and drove up and down country roads, rubbernecking across the broad, billowing plains where you could see so far it seemed you should spot the earth's curve. At last we sighted a man in a pasture, carrying a small rifle.

"Well now," said Dahlberg, as he pulled over and parked by the ditch.

The man, who was walking our way, paused a second at the sight of us, then came on.

It was Rex. He stared at me and then Dahlberg. Standing sober in sunlight he didn't have the mean look I remembered in the dance hall. His hair was tousled some and moved loose in the prairie wind. The sun had reddened his face and made his nose shiny. He looked young and vulnerable.

I studied the rifle, a small, bolt-action single shot. The kind that's only worth carrying if you know how to shoot very well.

"Get any?" I asked.

"Only the ones I saw," he answered and turned his attention on Dahlberg. "You looking for me?"

Dahlberg said yes and explained why.

It wasn't obvious but I thought I sensed he was relieved by the question about someone else. He tilted his head as he answered.

"I went around to see Dewey Saturday but he was working and didn't have any time. We didn't talk much. He didn't say anything about going anyplace."

"How long's it been since you saw him last before Saturday?"

"Close to a year. We sort of lost contact."

"You weren't buddies, huh?" said Dahlberg.

He shrugged. "You grow up."

"So how come all of a sudden you looked him up?"

"Didn't have anything better to do."

"Where you think he might've gone to?"

"I can't figure. Seems I heard there was a brother in California but they weren't close as I remember. Doesn't seem likely he'd take off sudden to visit him."

"We got reason to think his alibi for you was a phony," said Dahlberg. "Was it?"

Rex's mouth sagged for a second and then he scowled and the mean was back again.

"Who told you that?"

"Who'd know?"

"Oh, that's it, huh? You're trying to make out I did something to Dewey?"

"It's a notion that comes to mind under the circumstances.

So if you know where Dutro is you better tell us right now."

"I don't know and that's a goddamn fact. And I don't believe he ratted—"

"He had a girlfriend . . ." said Dahlberg and let it hang.

If it hadn't been for the sunburn I think Rex would have turned pale.

"What's she got to do with anything—"

"Seems like she told a fella she knew that the night you were supposed to be with Dewey, he was screwing this girl and you weren't around."

Rex sneered. "And I suppose you know where this screwing girlfriend is—"

"We just might, now let's go into town. I think we better talk a little more."

Rex clutched the twenty-two. "No. I'm not going."

"You gonna resist arrest? Great. Better'n a confession."

"You didn't say anything about arrest—you said we were gonna talk—"

"If you don't come willing, it'll be the hard way. That what you want?"

He took a deep breath and lowered the carbine until it was dangling from his right hand.

"No. I got nothing to worry about. I'll come along."

He gave Dahlberg the rifle and climbed into the front passenger seat. I sat behind him. He didn't look at all like a man with nothing to worry about.

12

DAHLBERG AND HIS captain hadn't been questioning Rex more than fifteen minutes when a lawyer showed up claiming the young man was his client and demanding to see him.

I guessed that Beulah had called Marvel the moment we left the farmhouse.

The lawyer brought the questioning to a quick whoa and after some chatter with Dahlberg, I traced McGinty through the hardware store to the local café, joined him for lunch, and we headed back home.

After I'd filled Mac in on the day's activities, we agreed we should try to run down the woman who'd shot Rex's alibi in talk with Jim Baltz.

Mac knew only two relatives of Lorraine Knight. There was an alcoholic father and a simpleminded younger brother. The father worked part-time at the local hotel when he was sober. The younger brother worked for a farmer not far from where Beulah Kruger lived.

On Friday morning I visited the father who was ashamed of his daughter and claimed he didn't know any of her friends and didn't want to. I located the brother, Timmy, early in the afternoon. The farmhouse was almost as dilapidated as the barn and I was directed to a pasture where he was busy repairing a barbed wire fence that'd been flattened by a falling elm during a recent windstorm.

He was shy at first but warmed quickly—obviously it wasn't often that anyone showed interest in anything he'd have to say. I took shameless advantage, asking more questions than necessary and taking in everything he had to say. I didn't figure it would hurt his sister or him any so it wasn't too unfair.

He told me Lorraine's closest friend was Prudence Fitz, daughter of the local grocery store proprietor. She worked the cash register there. If Timmy had it right, Lorraine and Prudence kept nothing from each other.

Despite the name I liked Prudence at first sight. She was talking with a hefty old party who was bitching about milk being raised from eight to ten cents a quart. Prudence agreed that was tough but pointed out that eggs were now down to eleven cents a dozen so she could stay about even if she drank less and ate more. The lady didn't seem to find that encouraging but she didn't have a counterargument and left looking thoughtful.

"What can I do for you?" Prudence asked me in a tone that made her sound like being helpful was her whole purpose in life.

I asked for a bag of Bull Durham; she handed it over with a package of papers and took my change.

"I'd like something else," I said.

Her quick gray eyes met mine for a split second before she grinned. Her face had dimples, clean skin, a small nose, and a wide mouth full of teeth worth showing off.

"So tell me," she said.

"I need information."

"I'm loaded," she assured me, "ask."

"You keep in touch with your friend Lorraine Knight?"

The grin didn't waver. "Who?"

"Okay," I said, "how about a young fella named Timmy Knight. He works on a farm north of town."

The grin faded some. "Yes, I know Timmy."

"Nice boy, right?"

"Timmy's about as nice as people get. Why?"

"He told me you were Lorraine's best friend. He wouldn't kid me, would he?"

She considered me solemnly. "You're the fellow from Corden, aren't you? The sign painter who works on mysteries."

"That's right."

"Why question Timmy?"

"You know Dewey Dutro?"

She nodded.

"He's disappeared. Nobody knows where or why. He talked with his girl night before last and didn't tell her anyplace he was going, but the next day he didn't show up for work and it looks like he never went home that night. He's the guy who gave Rex Tobler his alibi for the night when Genevieve Sinclair was murdered. It's important to find him—first to be sure he's okay, and second to see if he still wants to give Rex an alibi."

"What's all this got to do with Lorraine?"

"Lorraine told someone the alibi was phony. That Dewey spent that night with her, not drinking and playing cards with Rex. She ever tell you that?"

The gray eyes studied me a second before she said no.

"She ever run around with Dewey?"

"You mean did he ever make her, don't you?"

"That'd be worth knowing—but I'd settle for finding out if she was close enough so she'd have any notion where he'd have run off to—if he hasn't been murdered."

That reached her. She blinked and looked toward the store entrance a moment. When she spoke it was almost in a whisper.

"You think it's that bad?"

"How does it sound to you?"

"I can't believe it."

"Could you believe Genevieve was murdered when it happened?"

"No," she admitted.

"Look, I'm not gonna try and drag her back here—I just want to talk to her, even if it's only on the phone. You know where she is?"

She thought a moment and straightened her back.

"Where could she call you?"

"I'll hang around the hotel this evening. She can reach me after seven."

"All right," she said. "Be kind. She's had a rough time and she's a very nice girl. She's just always been weak with guys."

"I'd like to ask you another question about somebody else."

She raised her smooth eyebrows.

"You know if Rex had a regular woman in Aberdeen?"

"What made you think of that?"

"He strikes me as a guy who'd always be on the prowl. If he went to Aberdeen whenever he had a little problem, I'd guess he'd manage to line something up, to make it cozy."

"Well, I don't know anything for sure, but you're probably right. Lorraine mentioned something about a woman he was involved with. You might ask her."

I assured her I would and asked if she was in the store every day. She said yes. I said I'd see her. She didn't glow at the thought but her smile wasn't exactly discouraging.

13

LORRAINE KNIGHT CALLED a little after 8:00 P.M. Her voice had a muffled sound, as though she were holding the mouthpiece far away. She told me this had to be short because she couldn't afford long-distance calls. I said I'd pay the charges to Prudence and send them to her.

That brought her voice suddenly clearer.

"What a great idea—Pru said she thought you'd be nice—but can I trust you?"

"Yeah, but I don't know how to prove it. She tell you about Dewey and his disappearance?"

"Uh-huh. That sounds spooky to me. Dewey's a fella that gets all upset when he messes up. Like when he overslept a couple times and his boss, Mr. Brattman, called him at home, real disappointed in him, it just tore up Dewey something awful. He'd never just run off and not tell Mr. Brattman."

"Was Dewey with you the night Genevieve got killed?"

"Uh-huh. That was our first time all night. It was the first time all night for me ever. Him too, he said. We thought we were really in love. We were going to get married."

"Do you know if Rex had a girlfriend in Aberdeen?"

"Oh sure. That's the reason he wanted Dewey to say he was with Rex that night. Rex couldn't tell who he was really with because it was this married woman and he couldn't let anybody know about that. I mean, he'd rather have people think he was a murderer than have his lady exposed as an adulteress. Rex has a very high sense of honor and he's nuts about her."

"So how come Dewey knew about her?"

"He found out sort of by accident. I never knew how. In fact, Dewey didn't really want to talk to me about it because Rex was so weird about this woman."

"Did Genevieve know about the married woman?"

"I'm not real sure. One of the other guys crazy for Gen might've tipped her off. I bet they did. I'm pretty sure some of them knew about Rex's affair."

"Who'd be most likely?"

"Probably Mutt. He was the guy everybody confided in. And he was crazy about Genevieve, probably more than any of them. I mean, he like worshiped her."

"That's Mutt O'Keefe?"

"Uh-huh. He was Dewey's really closest pal and never liked Rex much. They all ran around together but you know how that goes."

"How well did you know Gen?"

"Oh, we were never friends. In the first place Pru and I were a year ahead of her in school and for another she was pretty stuck-up. She thought working for the Toblers made her family or something. The only girlfriend she had was that virgin princess, Holly, who was too good for any of the fellas."

"You said you and Dewey thought about getting married. What happened?"

"Well, I met Terry and just really fell in love. Terry was older and lots smarter about girls than Dewey. He made me feel like nothing in the world was more important than me and he couldn't live without me. So, we ran away. It was so romantic."

"It turned out okay, huh?"

"No. When I got pregnant and big he left me. It was very tragic. Will you really pay for this call? It's going to cost an awful lot—"

"Yes. Will you tell me where you are?"

"No. I won't be dragged back to Greenhill. I've got a good job now and a new fellow who's good to me and I'm not giving anything up. I just called because Dewey was nice to me and I did him wrong and don't want anything awful happening to him."

I thanked her for calling and she said don't mention it and hung up after reminding me I'd promised to pay for the call.

Saturday morning I was back painting signs and a bit before noon drifted over to the grocery store. Prudence was talking with a skinny older guy behind the counter. He had deep wrinkles that ran down the edge of his nostrils, framing his mouth and giving him a disapproving look, but his eyes were kind and they took me in as his daughter introduced us. I was surprised to learn he was her father since he looked old enough to be a grandpa. He didn't say anything about having heard of me, which I took as a good sign, and pretty soon he drifted off toward the back of the store.

"Lorraine any help?" asked Prudence.

"Quite a lot. Like you said, a nice girl. What I've really got to find out is who the married woman is in Aberdeen. What do you do about lunch?"

"I go home."

"How about going with me to the Do Drop Inn? I'll buy."

"That's the best proposition I've had all week. Come to think of it, it's the only decent one. Why not?"

She went to tell her father where she was going, came back, and we took off.

"How well do you know Mutt O'Keefe?" I asked when we were seated in a booth near the kitchen and had ordered our meals.

"Ah," she said, "so you're taking me to lunch for what I know, not because you're romantic."

"Actually I'm working to throw you off guard, like a feint, you know?"

"That sounds nice. Yes, I know Mutt. He's a good kid. Is that what you want to know?"

"Lorraine said he was Dewey's closest friend. That he might have told him about the woman in Aberdeen. The one Rex was trying to protect."

"If Lorraine said that, it's probably so. She's not the smartest girl I've ever known, but she seems able to understand everything about guys except how to keep them from taking advantage of her."

"You ever dated Mutt?"

"A couple times. No fireworks."

"Could you help me convince him that something's happened to his old buddy and we've got to know who this woman in Aberdeen is to settle Rex's involvement with Gen's murder?"

The waitress delivered our orders while Prudence stared at me in silence. When we were alone once more she said, "You know, Mr. Wilcox, I'm beginning to think you're a calculating so-and-so. You want me to do your work for you."

"I haven't asked you to paint a sign. That's my work. This is a town problem. Your town, your people. A guy everybody likes might be dead because too many people've been more worried about not making trouble than in solving a cold-blooded murder that's everybody's business. Which reminds me, I've got to give you money to pay for your girlfriend's call."

She stared for a moment when I handed over two ones, then calmly tucked them in her purse, picked up her knife and fork, and started on the hot beef sandwich. I tried my ham on rye.

After a moment she swallowed and met my eyes.

"Okay. I'm convinced. Tell me how you think I should go about this."

14

"YOU GOING TO the dance tonight?" I asked.

"Are you inviting me?"

"You got it."

"I'll go."

"Mutt comes, doesn't he?"

"Always."

"And he'll ask you for a dance."

"You know everything, don't you?"

"I don't know the name of Rex's woman in Aberdeen."

"All right," she said, brushing her mouth with a paper napkin, "if Mutt knows, I'll try to get it out of him. If he doesn't, or won't tell, do I have to pay you back for the dance?"

"No, you'll suffer enough just dancing with me."

She laughed and said I should pick her up at 8:30, and gave me her address. Then she returned to work at the store and I went back to sign painting.

It was the hottest day yet. The temperature hit over 100 by 2:30 and the fan was blowing air hot enough to singe hair. I gave up by 3:00 when McGinty came around and recommended beers at Manner's Bar.

The bar was some cooler than the hall where I'd been working. We sat at a table in a corner, me with my back to the wall, McGinty facing me.

"You going to the dance tonight?" he asked.

"Thought I might."

"Watch yourself," he said.

"What've you heard?"

"Some muttering. Nothing real clear. All's I know for sure is, strangers in town dancing with local girls are never what you'd call popular, you know?"

I knew it damned well.

"Anybody special?" I asked.

McGinty looked over his shoulder and leaned forward.

"I know Speed Wickert's in town. He's a halfback with the Minnesota Gophers. Grew up here. Stocky, quick. I'd guess some of the boys'd try to egg him into a go with you."

I settled for the one beer and went back to the hotel. Officer Schoop came around to chin about progress if any. When I finished telling about the talk with Lorraine he asked did I plan to hit the dance. I nodded.

"I was gonna suggest maybe you stay away from the dance hall tonight. There could be some trouble."

"This football player, Speed Wickert?"

"Where'd you hear that?"

I told about McGinty's tip.

"Speed's okay," he said, "but he gets kinda wild when he drinks. I think playing football's leveled him a little. He don't have to throw his weight around to show he's a big little man anymore. Everybody knows it. But you never know. I'll be at the hall much as I can. Just be careful, okay?"

I promised him I would and he suggested we have dinner together so's people'd know how things were. I wasn't too crazy about that but agreed.

"It was 8:28 P.M. as I approached the Fitz home. The sun

was way low, the wind had dropped, and the temperature probably wasn't more than about 97. I had my clean white shirt on
with the sleeves up a double fold and had even brushed off my
shoes some. Prudence came to the door in a white sleeveless
dress with matching shoes and silk stockings.

"You look like a million bucks," I told her.

"It's just a little something I sewed up through most of the
winter. You look clean, and for a furry man, don't seem to sweat
much."

I wasn't sure whether that was a crack at my open collar or
the rolled-up sleeves but of course she couldn't miss the hair on
the back of my hands even if I'd been in a suit and tie.

It was no more than four blocks to the dance hall and we
ambled along the quiet sidewalk under occasional elms and box
elders that stirred easy in the gentle wind.

"Where'll you go when you leave Greenhill?" she asked.

"Probably Ipswich."

"Why not Aberdeen?"

"Too big. I like towns between one and two thousand, where
there's no local sign painters. You can get known quick and pick
up leads easy."

"Don't you get tired of traveling?"

"Not yet."

"I don't think I'd like it. It's nice to live in a town where you
know nearly everybody and everybody knows you and there's a
sense of real belonging."

I don't believe anybody really knows himself, let alone the rest,
but I didn't figure it was a subject for this night, or maybe any other.

I asked how come she didn't have a steady.

"Well, I sort of do. There's this boy I went with through my
senior year in high school. He's a student at the University of
Missouri—in journalism. He's doing awfully well and got a job
working for a small-town newspaper near Columbia and he's
going to be there all summer and then go to his senior year at the

university. We write letters a lot. At least I do. He's awfully busy."

"Will he be sore if he hears about me taking you to the dance?"

"Oh no. He told me I could go with other fellows. He's very self-confident and has great faith in our relationship."

I figured he was either a conceited ass or a damned indifferent lover. Or had plans elsewhere. Probably all three.

There were a few kids already dancing when we made our way into the dance hall. We got our hands stamped after I paid the fifty-cent admission. The band was one I'd seen and heard in Corden a time or two and I remembered their drummer was good enough to play solos a couple times a night while the crowd gathered around and just watched him sweat. I had the feeling if he went all out in the heat of this night it might be his last.

Prudence introduced me to a couple girlfriends and we just watched the finish of a couple numbers before they played one that sounded tame enough for me to handle. All the while I was rubbernecking around, trying to spot the kind of gang that'd be working something up. Everything looked pretty innocent.

Prudence was light on her feet and moved any which way I guided her and things were going very good. I decided this was a dandy woman.

Mutt O'Keefe showed up near 9:30 and got around to Prudence pretty quick. I found Holly and asked for a dance. While we moved around I glanced over at Prudence and Mutt once too often and Holly asked was I stuck on her. I couldn't think of a bright response to that and just laughed and asked who'd she come to the dance with.

She said Speed Wickert.

I thought, uh-oh.

When the number ended I walked her over to the west wall where there were folding chairs used by the girls. Like at dances all over our territory, the girls sat between numbers and guys stood.

I looked around, saw three guys pretty well surrounding Prudence, and moved toward her. A guy backed in front of me and I barely brushed him as I slipped by. He grabbed my upper arm and pulled me around.

"Hey, Buster," he said, "you better watch where I'm going."

"When you don't know, it's hard for me to tell," I said.

He was a hair or two taller than me, a good deal wider, and had the slab jaw and thick neck of an athlete. I could smell booze and knew the glitter in his pale blue eyes.

"Don't ask Holly for another dance," he said.

I smiled at him. "You want to fight, right?"

"Anytime, buster. Let's just go around back—"

"I got a better idea. You want to fight with me it'll be for real. We'll go in my car or yours, a mile out of town. The guy who can drive back's the winner. You got the guts to fight without your gang at your back?"

There was a second's doubt in the cold eyes, then he looked me up and down and grinned.

"Why not?"

"Hey," a nearby friend told him, "be careful—"

"I can handle him," said the scrappy one. "We'll go in my crate."

I didn't see Schoop around as we walked out of the front door and left to a green Chevy parked diagonally at the curb. We climbed in, he started it up, backed out, and headed west.

"So," I said, "you're Speed Wickert, the football hero."

"Uh-huh. And you're Wilcox, the hobo part-time cop."

"Who suckered you into this fight?" I asked.

"You're the detective, Wilcox, you figure it out."

"It wasn't Rex, he's still in Aberdeen, so it was just some local sap who wanted you to punch the guy he was afraid to try."

We reached a turn-off, which he swung into, then he braked us to a standstill and said this'd do.

We got out opposite sides and met in front of the car.

"Might's well do it here," he said, "I don't want to have to carry you too far when we're through."

He came in a rush; I made as if to meet him and at the last second ducked under. He wasn't as drunk as I'd like—he managed to grab my belt as I rose under him and hung in when he started flight so we both wound up rolling on the ground. He was up quick as a cat and we circled each other a moment before he feinted a shot to the head. I grabbed for it and he counterpunched one meant for my gut, but it hit my ribs and tilted me. I let myself drop, he stumbled on top, I rolled him off, and when he came up leading with his chin I clipped him dandy right and left. He staggered, covered, and backed off. I let him go and waited.

"You really want to fight?" I asked. "What's the percentage?"

He moved in. We both threw punches but kept them tight and did no damage.

"You don't need a broken nose or busted teeth," I said, "not fighting with nobody watching and a season of football left."

He bobbed and weaved, feinted punches, tried to crowd me, feinted a charge, and finally came on. I speared him on the nose, took a punch on the side of my head, and when he was in close hooked him in the gut a good one.

We clinched, staggered around, and I managed to trip him. He tried wrestling and wound up with my elbow in his gut and a head butt to his chin.

"You having fun?" I asked. "What's the damned point?"

He tried two more flurries and when we both backed off, puffing like crazy, he suddenly dropped his hands and started laughing.

"Shit," he said, "you're right. You willing to call it a draw?"

"Bet your ass. We'd beat each other's ears off we kept on."

"You're the toughest bastard I've ever met my size," he said. "I should've known when I grabbed your damned arm in the dance hall. Let's go back to town. I'll buy you a beer."

15

ON THE WAY back I asked Speed who'd egged him into calling me out and he said there were several guys but it didn't mean anything. Anytime a new guy was in town it was likely to happen. Especially if he moved in on local girls and absolutely when he started stirring things up.

"From all I hear," he said, "you're a hell of a stirrer."

"Was Jim Baltz one of the guys?"

"Hey, there's no reason to get sore at any of them. We got it settled, okay?"

I said good enough and asked if he'd known Genevieve.

"Only enough to remember what she looked like. Cute kid. Flirty. I was a year ahead of her. Seniors never messed with girls from the junior class."

I asked if he had any notions about the murder and he admitted that it didn't mean all that much to him.

"You leave a town like Greenhill and go to Minneapolis, you lose touch in a hurry, you know? Listen, we both look like hell, let's go by my folks' place and clean up. I can loan you a shirt and you brush off your pants while I change into fresh stuff."

His parents had gone to the movie so we had the house to

ourselves and he talked steady. Yeah, he had known Lorraine Knight, no he hadn't been in her pants but knew Dewey had and maybe a couple others before she ran off with Bock.

"There were enough guys in line wanting her that if any-body'd had a clue Bock would run off with her there'd been a lynching, you bet. She was really a sweet piece."

I asked how long he'd been interested in Holly and he said from the first time he saw her but her being a junior when he was a senior he'd not had the balls to ask her out. Now of course that didn't make any difference especially with him being known as a star with the Gophers. Not that it'd done him any good so far. Her idea of going all the way was a good-night kiss at the door. "And nobody's got any further than me," he said with confidence.

It was near 11:30 when we got back to the dance hall after a quick beer at Manner's Bar. I saw Prudence in one of the folding chairs, with Mutt O'Keefe standing by her side. She came to her feet as I approached and stared at my face angrily.

"What happened—where'd you go?"

"Had a conference with Speed Wickert," I said. "Sorry it took so long."

"They said you'd gone to fight—you did, didn't you? Your cheek's swollen and your nose looks scuffed. . . ."

"You should see the other guy."

She looked past me and I turned to see Speed talking with Holly. She looked annoyed when I first saw her but after Speed said something she smiled and then even laughed.

I asked Prudence if she'd dance with a brawler and she said she guessed so since I was the guy that brung her.

"What'd you get from Mutt?" I asked.

"The woman's name is Delancy. Norma Delancy. Her husband owns a hardware store in Aberdeen."

"You're terrific. How'd you manage it?"

"I told him you asked me and why I thought he should help you. I didn't lie a word."

I gave her a squeeze and told her she was well named.

"Well, Mutt's such a nice guy I couldn't be anything but honest with him. And he's the sort of fellow who appreciates that. Why'd you get Speed to drive out of town for the fight?"

"That's real simple. First, if we started a brawl here, Schoop would try to stop it. And second, it's never too good fighting the local hero in the middle of his friends, and when you get him off he knows the fight's for real, not a show. But most of all, that way I could talk sense to him and hope he was smart enough to catch some of it when he started getting winded."

"It must have taken a while, you both look beat."

"It did. If it'd lasted much longer I'd have to been damned dirty to win—he's awful young and in good shape."

"I was worried," she said. "Mutt told me he wasn't drunk at all—just had one before they came to the dance."

"Yeah, I guessed that early on. You mind if we move out and have something at the café? I don't need a lot more exercise."

The number we were dancing to ended as we moved toward the door and the band started playing "Marie." Prudence stopped me.

"Would you mind awfully waiting this one out? I promised I'd dance with Jim Baltz when they played this—he made a request—"

"Go ahead," I said. "But ask him if he was one of the guys who egged Speed into trying me."

She rolled her eyes and moved off.

Just as I was about to lean against a support post, Steffi, who was sitting with a group of wallflowers, caught my eye with a wistful look.

I went over.

"You told me you were a good dancer," I said. "Want to prove it?"

She grinned as she got up. "I told you I wasn't bad."

She wasn't quite up to Prudence but she was fine enough

and we moved around the floor nice and easy. When we were doing our bit in the end of the hall away from the gawkers she pulled my head down and suggested we dance more over where everybody could see us. She smiled serenely as I went along and at the end gave me a head bob and said I wasn't bad either but I should learn fancier steps. I told her I try hard never to over-reach.

As I walked Prudence toward the café she said it was sweet of me to dance with Steffi.

"You absolutely made the night for her," she said.

"She told me I should learn fancier steps."

That about cracked Prudence up. When we were in a booth she told me Steffi was horribly competitive and couldn't help trying to put me in my place. I said that was pretty plain even to me. Then I asked if she'd learned anything from Jim Baltz.

She said he denied having anything to do with siccing Speed on me and claimed nobody else had as far as he knew.

"You believe him?"

"No. Did you ask Speed himself?"

"Yeah. He said forget it, didn't mean a thing. The murder doesn't mean anything to him either. It's not real because Genevieve was in a class behind him and didn't count."

"Isn't that sad? Most of us are like that, I'm afraid."

16

SUNDAY WAS CLEAR and hot. After breakfast at the inn I borrowed a Montgomery Ward catalog from the hotel manager and picked out a new tent with a lean-to shelter for the Model T. It went for $17.50 and I figured by the end of my sign painting I could afford to order it.

Then I got in my Model T, wheeled to the lake, and parked by the fallen cottonwood where I'd gone swimming and had dinner the last time. The wind made waves and occasional whitecaps flashed white on the deep blue water. I hiked along the wide beach to a slough on the south side which had been a shallow lake a couple years back. Red-winged blackbirds darted around over the cattails and grungy mud hens paddled lazily, peering into the brackish water. Most of the other waterfowl had disappeared. The drought hadn't noticeably bothered bugs any and they kept the fancy blackbirds well fed and prolific.

A redwing turned feisty when I neared his nest and rose to dive at my head and squawk. I backed off, leaving him in charge. His kind were making their calls all over the place and it was sweet and comfortable.

Back near the fallen cottonwood I fished from shore but it was too shallow anywhere within reach and the hook gathered nothing but seaweed.

I returned to the hotel before noon, gave Prudence a call, and came up blank. Steffi answered when I tried for Holly and asked how I'd made out with Prudence last night.

"What kind of a question is that for a girl to ask?"

"Would it be okay if I was a guy?"

"It'd be none of your business either way but in case you're broadcasting, her folks were sitting on the porch when I walked her home so the good-nights were pretty formal."

"I could've told you it'd be like that," she said.

"So how'd Speed do with Holly?"

"She wouldn't even kiss him because he'd started that fight with you."

"She seemed to think he was funny at the dance hall."

"Oh, she laughed about it, but she was still put out. I don't suppose you called to talk with me?"

"You know everything, don't you?"

"I'm working on it. Hold on."

Holly said good morning in a distant tone and I asked if she was sore at me.

"Just a minute," she said and put her hand over the mouthpiece while she told Steffi to get lost. A moment later she was back.

"You were crazy to do what you did—what in the world were you thinking of when you drove off with Dale last night?"

"Dale?"

"Dale Wickert. You didn't think he was christened Speed, did you?"

"I've heard stranger ones. When did he ask you to go to the dance with him?"

"He telephoned long distance from Minneapolis on Thursday."

"You gone with him before?"

"A couple of times. I wasn't very impressed and I'm not quite sure why I accepted this time. Probably because it was rather flattering to be asked by long distance. I was surprised to see you with Prudence."

"She was going to give me some help on getting information, so I thought paying her way was the decent thing to do."

"What a proper fellow you are. Did she find out what you wanted to know?"

"Maybe. Did Speed tell you who put him up to the little fracas last night?"

"I never asked. Probably it just popped into his own thick head."

"Two people warned me to expect something from him before I went to the dance. It sounded like a setup. When did Speed get to town?"

"Friday night, I think. I'm pretty sure. Are you suggesting that he came to Greenhill on somebody's invitation just to start a fight with you? That's not very flattering for me."

"Well, it'd be pretty flattering for me, but I can't help but wonder. I got the notion he hadn't spent a lot of time home since he went off to college."

She said that was certainly true and was silent a moment while we both thought things over.

"You going to see him again?" I asked.

"Nothing's set. He said he'd call and I told him not to bother. I don't really care for his type. Are you about to suggest I go with him and get answers for you?"

"Well, you'd be a good one to find out who his close buddies are. Was he ever buddy-buddy with Rex?"

"Not that I know of."

"How'd you feel if I called Speed and suggested he invite you to go swimming with Prudence and me at the lake south of town this afternoon?"

She was silent for a few seconds. Finally she said I must think she was really determined to find out who killed Genevieve. I admitted the notion stuck in my mind.

"Have you already asked Prudence?"

"No. I called the house but suppose everybody went to church."

"Probably. We're about the only heathens in town. Okay, if you can line up Prudence or anybody else I'll expect to hear from Speed."

It sold easy as beer on Saturday night. We went in Speed's car, which was a four-door, and he picked a beach I'd not seen, on the north side of the lake.

I hate to admit how satisfying it was seeing Speed's face looking lots worse for wear than mine. He told our partners the fight had really been even—he just looked worse because I'd never looked good. Holly seemed to think that was funny. Prudence had better taste.

Both girls looked good in their bathing suits; Holly was long-legged and smooth, Prudence more rounded and compact. We hit the water quick and it felt great after the hot sun. I swam straight out and rolled on my back to admire the blue sky for a few seconds. There wasn't a cloud. The horizons looked pale, as if the hot sun had faded most of the blue out. I heard the girls laughing at something Speed said and swam back but never found out what was so funny. We stretched out on blankets spread over the sand and took in sun while they chattered, mostly about school friends and past dances. Holly brought it around to Genevieve's murder.

Speed said it had to have been done by somebody from a neighboring town. He couldn't accept the notion of anybody he knew did it. He admitted, when Holly pressed him, that Rex had a reputation for a terrible temper but insisted he couldn't have killed Genevieve.

"Why're you so positive?" I asked. "Because of his married woman in Aberdeen?"

That startled him too much to hide and at first he tried to play dumb. Neither of the girls bought it and both started in on him until they made him admit he'd heard there was a woman in Aberdeen. They both pooh-poohed him when he insisted he'd simply heard the story indirectly.

"Dale Wickert," said Holly, "I know you too well to believe you just swallowed a vague story about this woman. You know more and if you've any honor at all you'll tell enough so it can be settled once and for all whether Rex really has an alibi for that night."

"Okay, damn it. I know he was with Mrs. Delancy because Dewey, Mutt, and I were together that night and I drove him over to the back alley of her house and dropped him off and we saw her let him in the back door. And I picked him up at two A.M. Now, goddamn it, I've told you and if anybody spills it they'll be sorry."

"Lorraine Knight says she was with Dewey all that night," I said.

"She was. I took Dewey over to her place right after dropping off Rex."

17

WE WANTED TO know why the hell all that crowd had driven Rex to his woman's house. Speed explained they had been together drinking wine that Mutt O'Keefe got from an older friend, and somebody suggested they go to a whorehouse. Rex had backed off and when they called him yellow he got mad and told them he had a date with a rich married woman and wouldn't mess with whores.

"Of course, we all hooted at that till he lost his temper and said he'd damned well show us and he gave me the address and said drive down the alley, let him out, and watch.

"So we did and he strutted up to the back door of this big house and after a couple seconds this woman let him in and hugged him, and then he closed the door. I went back to get him two hours later, like he asked.

"He wouldn't tell us a damned thing more and it was plain he was sorry he'd let anybody know about what he had going. Rex always hated it when he got drunk, lost his temper, and did something dumb like that."

"How'd you find out her name?" I asked.

"Dewey recognized her because his boss was one of

Delancy's Saturday morning coffee buddies and he'd seen her with him lots of times. He'd always wondered why in hell this great-looking young woman had married such an old bastard."

"How'd Rex meet Mrs. Delancy?" I asked.

He had no idea and said he didn't think anybody knew because after that time he'd never mentioned her to any of the guys again.

A sudden storm came out of the southeast and we scrambled to the car and were still driving toward town when it hit. First there was dust when the wind came, then rain poured down so fierce we couldn't see through the windshield. Speed pulled off the road and waited it out. Ten minutes later it was over. We could see blue sky on the horizon by the time we reached Greenhill's city limits.

Prudence took me into her house and her ma looked a little shocked that we were in swimming outfits but took it okay when she realized we'd been chased from the beach by the storm. She was a small, stocky woman with her hair in a bun and bright blue eyes that worked me over. I didn't think she was nuts about her daughter messing with a guy my age, but she was polite and I guessed had better sense than to make anything of it to Prudence even in private.

When we were dressed and decent I thanked Prudence for her help.

"I think we should go talk with Mutt," she said.

"Why?"

"He's the only one Rex confided in. You want more details on his affair, Mutt's the only one who'd know. Tell you what, I'll call him up and we'll go see him tonight. Okay?"

It went fine.

He met us on the family front porch and led us around in back where his mother had a picnic table with benches and we sat there in the fading light of early evening.

He was plainly uncomfortable about my being with Prudence so I kept my mouth shut and left the questioning to her. She started slow and general.

"Didn't Rex work for his dad a couple summers?" she asked.

"Uh-huh. In the parts department of the garage. His old man wanted him to learn the business like from the bottom and Rex hated it. He didn't like getting his hands dirty and wearing work clothes and the guys didn't appreciate having the boss's son around. Rex thought they took him for a spy or something."

"But he stuck it out two summers?"

"Yeah. Then, year before last, he got a job as a used car salesman in Aberdeen. He did it on his own and his dad was sore about it and gave him fits."

"What happened this summer?"

"Well, he couldn't get the job back—he hadn't really been very good selling. An insurance company took him on but he hasn't done a lot there either. Al won't give him any money but his aunt does—he's always been a favorite of hers. He's been going out to her farm and doing chores now and again since he was little. Now he does it more so he can pretend he earns what she gives him."

Prudence talked a little about the problems of working for a person's parents and then, casually, asked where Rex first met Mrs. Delancy.

"At their hardware store. He'd spent Friday night at his aunt's place and came into town early Saturday morning to buy a new rake and a hoe and there was this woman clerk alone in the hardware store. He couldn't get over the notion of a woman working there and talking like she knew tools. He didn't find out until he mentioned her to his aunt that Norma was the store owner's wife. He managed to go back the next Saturday and she was alone again and he got talking with her when he was trying to pick a pocketknife. She was full of advice and he finally asked if she'd take some from him. She said about what and he said about her clothes; she ought to wear something that made more of her great figure. She told him he was fresh and he said she was a knockout and she laughed and said he was pretty cute himself.

"So he kept going back."

"Where was the husband Saturday mornings?"

"He met with a bunch of business cronies at the café a block down the street."

"Then what?"

"Well, it turned out she liked movies, her husband didn't, so she went alone and Rex started meeting her in movie theaters and then they'd go someplace in his car."

Prudence kept pressing him gently for more details and pretty soon, as if he were making a personal confession, Mutt began to unload.

The necking moved on to making love in the backseat and later they got so bold Rex went to the house after Delancy had gone to bed and they'd do it in the living room. Once her husband had an upset stomach and came downstairs looking for his wife. She barely hustled Rex into the basement and was in the kitchen adjusting her housecoat when he found her and wanted to know what she'd done with the Alka-Seltzer. She got him taken care of and back in bed and brought Rex out of the basement and they took up where they'd left off.

I asked how old Mrs. Delancy was and he said she was probably about three years older than Rex. Her father had been the partner of Delancy when their hardware store was first opened. Delancy's first wife died when Norma was in her early teens. A week after Norma's seventeenth birthday her parents died in a flash fire caused by a kerosene stove explosion in the kitchen. Norma pretty well went to pieces; Delancy took care of all the funeral arrangements, settled a sale of the house, and got her set up in a dinky apartment downtown. A year later they married.

According to Mutt, Rex claimed Norma never slept with her

husband. She had her own bedroom and was nothing more than a combination maid, cook, and bookkeeper for the old man. Rex had tried to coax her into leaving him but she wouldn't hear of it. Said she owed him too much to hurt him that way and if Rex loved her he'd wait. Delancy was old and frail; it wasn't likely he'd live long.

"Did that give Rex any ideas?" I asked.

Mutt stared at me. "What do you mean?"

"He ever think she was giving him a hint—that maybe he'd find a way to be sure the old man didn't last too long?"

Mutt looked at Prudence and shook his head. "This guy's sick."

She stared back at him and he looked away.

"Okay," I said, "that's got nothing to do with our problem so let's forget it. Have you ever met this Norma?"

"No. Rex didn't want her to know any of his friends had a notion who she was. She was supposed to be his secret all the way. It made him feel real guilty telling me everything but he said if he couldn't talk to me he'd bust—he couldn't keep it all inside."

"How long had this thing with Norma been going on when Gen got killed?"

"About half a year, I guess."

"You think Norma knew anything about Rex dating Gen?"

He said he had no way of knowing but it didn't seem too likely. Norma never went anyplace where she'd pick up gossip about Greenhill high school kids.

"She ever drive a car?"

He didn't know. According to Rex, when they got together outside her house it was always in Rex's car. Or rather, his father's.

When we had all I thought we could milk from Mutt I walked Prudence back home. The porch was unoccupied and we sat down on the wicker lounge and talked over what we'd heard.

"I've got to talk with Norma Delancy," I said.

"You think maybe she'd be easy?"

"To talk with?"

"To get to bed."

"Never thought of it," I lied.

"I'll bet."

I tried another direction.

"You seemed to agree with me that maybe she was trying to give Rex ideas about doing in her hubby."

She leaned back and lifted her chin a moment before looking at me once more.

"Like you said, it doesn't make much difference, does it? The old man's still alive as far as we know. But what you're after is the character of Norma, right? Did she maybe know about Gen and Rex being cozy and could she have been the one to kill Genevieve? If that was the case, he might be willing to take the blame for her because he'd feel he'd driven her to it. That assumes he's as buggy about her as Mutt thinks and since the affair has dragged over four years maybe he's right."

The problem was, how to meet Mrs. Delancy. It looked like I'd have to go visit Aberdeen again.

18

THE BRIEF RAINSTORM Sunday didn't relieve the heat and the hall where I worked was a giant oven by Monday noon. It seemed enough to make the paints bubble. McGinty was too smart to come around but was in the Do Drop Inn when I stopped by for lunch, and cheerfully informed me I looked like I needed a cold shower.

"What I'm gonna do," I said, "is hit the lake once this meal settles."

He said it must be lovely to work only when the spirit moved you and I told him he should be an expert on the subject.

Mayor Sullivan had paid me Friday for my week's labors (less the advance he'd made) and I decided this time the trip to Aberdeen would be on my own with no company or pay for mileage. And nobody knowing my plans.

I hit the lake enough to get the stink off before driving to Aberdeen and put on the white shirt Speed loaned me Saturday night so I wouldn't look too scruffy for a man going to the big city.

Monday afternoon in downtown Aberdeen was almost as dead as Corden or Greenhill. Most of the stores were one- and two-floor affairs, the street was wide and not many cars were parked along the curbs, with most of them being the usual Fords and Chevies but also some Buicks and Oldsmobiles, a few Dodges and Hudsons, and one sparkling new Graham Page.

I parked diagonally on the main drag and wandered along the sidewalk to Delancy's Hardware. After gawking at lawn mowers, tool kits, and hoses displayed in the windows out front, I went up the single step to the entry and through the open door. It was cool and seemed dark until my eyes adjusted. A boy, about seventeen, came my way with a worried look on his downy face and asked if he could help. I told him I wanted to look at their supply of paintbrushes and paints. He nodded seriously and led me to the rear, right-hand side of the store and waved at the shelves and drawers. I said fine, I'd nose around a little if he didn't mind. He looked something between relieved and doubtful, but nodded brightly and wandered off. I looked around for Norma, didn't see her at first, and figured it'd be just my luck to come around when she was taking some time off.

It was lucky I didn't need any brushes because they had none I could use. I moved on to the wall where they displayed carpenter tools and was gawking when I sensed the clerk moving close and glanced around.

Instead of the boy, I was looking at a well-curved woman with brown hair cut in a short bob. Her lips were thin, the cheeks round and rouged. A high brow and strong chin made her head seem large. Her smile was wide, warm, and sparkling.

She asked if she could help. I said she sure could if she was Mrs. Delancy.

"I am. What do you want?"

"I need to know some things about a friend of yours, Rex Tobler."

I didn't expect her to faint or turn white but thought the name would make her nervous about the young clerk hearing. She didn't even blink.

"What things?"

"It'd probably be better if we could talk somewhere more private."

There was a noticeable flicker in the large dark eyes, which she tried to hide by turning her head as the young clerk greeted a familiar customer by name near the front of the store.

She turned back to me and said, "You must be that man, Carl Wilcox."

"So Rex has been talking to you. Did he say I beat him up?"

"No. He said you'd probably be bothering me."

"Can we talk?"

"I suppose I've no choice." She glanced around at the customer and young clerk. The customer was talking.

"I've been talking with friends of Rex," I said. "They claim you could keep him from being the favorite suspect in a murder done four years back. You interested?"

"We can talk by telephone," she said. "Sometime after five. I go home to get dinner started before my husband gets there."

I thanked her and left.

The day stayed hot but the wind blew strong and kept me from sweating as I roamed the town. In a drugstore phone booth I looked up the Delancy address and then hiked over to the house. It was on a side street, about the middle of the block, a little larger than average but not showy. A high privy hedge gave the backyard exceptional privacy and a garage stood parallel with the alley. I walked to the garage apron and saw it would be no problem sighting on the kitchen entry from a car in the alley.

Just after five I rang her number. She answered on the first ring.

"What's Rex told you about me?" I asked.

"Not much more than that you seem to be persecuting him. I don't understand why you're involved in this."

"Al Schoop, the Greenhill cop, asked me to help find out who killed Genevieve. Things have come up that make it plain that alibi Rex gave for that night was phony. Dewey, the guy who gave him the alibi, has disappeared and I've talked with a woman who says she spent that night with Dewey and Rex was nowhere around. Others have said they saw Rex go into your house that night. I understand why you haven't come forward and why Rex hasn't named you. What I want to nail down is, was he with you?"

"And if I say he was, then what?"

"Then it'll be plain he couldn't have killed her. And neither could you."

"Me?"

"Did you know he'd been involved with Genevieve?"

"Of course not!'

"You didn't hear he'd made her pregnant and she was trying to force him into marrying her?"

"That's ridiculous!"

I let that sit a moment and she waited me out.

"So you never heard of Genevieve?"

"Well," she admitted, "I heard about some girl murdered—I guess that was her name."

"And Rex didn't tell you he was a suspect?"

"He said he was questioned but nobody really thought he did it and I didn't have to worry."

"You accepted that?"

"Well, no, I worried. But I knew he didn't do it, and it was all forgotten until you showed up."

"The Greenhill cop hadn't forgotten. Neither'd her family and most of the town."

"They would if you hadn't poked in."

"I was asked in—by Schoop. And most of the town is behind him. If it comes down to cases, would you give Rex his alibi?"

It took a moment for her to reply and when she did it was barely audible. I asked what she said.

"I don't know. What if nobody believed me? Then my reputation would be ruined and my husband would suffer for no good reason. . . ."

"And you wouldn't care if Rex got convicted?"

"Oh God, yes. Of course . . ."

"Okay. Good. Now, will you talk with me and help figure out who else might have done it? Was there anybody who'd like to frame Rex? How about your husband—maybe he got wise and planned to get rid of him, one way or another."

She made a sound that could have been a laugh.

"Buff's an old man who goes to bed by nine every night of his life and doesn't care about anything but having his meals on time, his clothes and house clean, and his store running efficiently. He never notices anything else. If he'd caught Rex and me together he'd have been shocked but he wouldn't go crazy mad or start plotting elaborate revenge. You want to meet him and see for yourself? Come over tonight. I'll tell him you're my cousin from Cleveland, just passing through. You can see what he's like."

"Fine. Does he smoke?"

"He likes a cigar now and then."

"What kind?"

"I don't know—nothing fancy."

"Okay. I'll come around eight, if that suits you."

"Yes. He won't suspect anything. He never remembers anything about my family."

I said good and hung up.

19

BUFORD DELANCY ANSWERED my knock and let me know at once his wife had never mentioned any cousin Carl. He wasn't suspicious or accusing, his attitude was one of resentment about being left uninformed.

I explained that we were far-removed cousins who'd never met so it was natural I'd not come up. He seemed satisfied when I explained that her uncle had told me what a fine woman she was and urged me to stop by when I passed through Aberdeen, so I did.

When I offered him a La Fendrich cigar it was plain he figured I was a gentleman, no matter the outward appearance, and he forgave his wife and me.

Norma gave me a sly grin as she headed for the kitchen after coffee, and Delancy began telling me what a friend his wife's father had been to him and how they had opened the first hardware store in Aberdeen and been like brothers.

"Better than brothers, as a matter of fact. Most brothers I've known fought like roosters. We never did. His death—and his wife with him—that was the greatest tragedy in my life. It didn't hurt that bad losing my own folks. I'll tell you, it was the naturalest thing in the world that their daughter and me married. We both loved them like life itself and just naturally had to stay together."

"She's a lucky girl," I said and didn't feel I was being hypocritical. She was lucky because he'd given her security and comfort and she'd still been able to enjoy a sex life that hadn't intruded on his or her peace of mind.

Yet.

"The best part," he told me, "is she appreciates that. I'll die and leave her still plenty young enough to marry a fella near her age—maybe younger, eh? And have a full, round life."

"You look like a guy might live forever," I told him.

He chuckled. "I certainly wouldn't wish that on her. You married?"

"No. Had a wife but lost her."

"Too bad," he said. "Man needs a wife. Maybe Norma can round up somebody but it ain't too likely. Doesn't have women friends. Working days and living with an old codger, she doesn't have much social life. I worry about that but she's content. Sweetest wife a man ever dreamed of—"

She carried in a coffee tray and told him to stop boring me bragging about her. He waved his big hand and laughed.

The coffee was weak and I wondered if she made it that way so he wouldn't stay too alert.

He asked me where I was heading and I said east and he assumed to the coast but didn't probe any more. He was one of those men who ask questions for sociability, not information.

Norma was different. She was a digger.

"I seem to remember hearing you were in the army," she said.

"Twice. Once during the World War and for another hitch a few years later—when I got sent to the Philippines."

She wanted details and really poked into the six months spent as a beachcomber after my discharge from service. She even asked what kind of discharge they gave me and I admitted it hadn't been honorable but avoided details because it was all old army crap that happened because I outfought the first sergeant. The charge was drunkenness. Hell, if every drinking GI got kicked out we'd never had an army big enough to whip Corden's Ladies Aid Society.

Around nine old Buford's eyes got heavy and pretty soon Norma was telling him to go to bed and like a perfect child he wished me good night and toddled off.

"Well," she said, "what do you think?"

"He couldn't be more convincing if you'd rehearsed him," I said.

She laughed, asked if I'd care for some sugar cookies, and getting my agreement, delivered. Then she sat at the edge of an easy chair, crossed her ankles, and cradled her coffee cup on her knees. This was a completely different woman from the one on the telephone and I guessed she had been talking with Rex before I arrived. Suddenly she was younger, friendly, almost confiding.

"Did Rex ever talk to you about his family?" I asked.

"Not a lot. He hates his father and is a little funny about his mother. I mean, while you could tell he admires her, he's always getting mad because she has to let everybody know how much smarter she is."

"Why's he hate his father?"

"I'm not sure. Maybe it's his bossiness and superiority. Rex isn't interested in the family business and despises the parts-shop job. Feels his father is trying to put him in his place, you know? Claims he treats the maid better than his son. Shows her more respect. He hates the way his father speaks to his mother at times. Like once he told her she looked like a potato sack tied in the middle."

Norma giggled. "I guess she does, but he shouldn't have said anything like that. I think Rex is jealous of his dad—because he's taller and so distinguished looking. Rex is always making fun of him posing like a king or something."

"What'd Rex tell you about me?"

She gave me a sideways look.

"He said you fought real dirty—butted him in the face with your head. He said he'd have beaten you if Schoop hadn't stopped the fight. In some ways, Rex is still a little boy. He couldn't admit even to himself anyone could beat him. But I could tell he's afraid of you and is terrified that you might make everybody believe he killed that girl. That whole business is driving him about crazy. Who told you about us?"

I ignored her question and asked if he'd said what caused our fight. She said he told her I'd bumped into him on the dance floor and he lost his temper and took a swing. Obviously he hadn't been dumb enough to let her know about his interest in the girl I'd been dancing with.

I asked what they had decided to do if he got charged with murdering Genevieve.

"We never really talked about it. He just won't accept the notion I might be dragged into it at all. But if it comes to Rex going to jail for something he didn't do, I'll have to come out."

"What about your husband?"

"It'll kill him, I suppose. But he's old and hasn't much more time anyway. I've given him five good years."

She stated that while watching closely for a reaction. If she was disappointed by my blank stare she hid it well with her smile. Sober, the lips looked thin and cold. Smiling, they radiated heat.

I asked if he ever talked about his friends.

"Not much," she said with a shrug. "Except for times when he complains about his parents we mostly just talk about each other and what we'll do when we're free of the old folks and can do as we please.

"I guess that makes us sound like a couple teenagers. That's what we were when we met and we've never quite got over it when we're together. I don't think Rex will ever get over it. Maybe that's why I love him so—he can be like a little boy."

She went to the door with me as I left and said, just before I went out, that it was awfully nice of me to bring Buford a cigar.

"He didn't smoke it."

"He will tomorrow, on his walk to work. I don't like cigar smoke so he never lights one at home."

It was all such a sweet domestic scent it bothered me and instead of getting into my jalopy and driving home I dropped around the police station and asked if Dahlberg might be on duty. The desk man said he might be but not at the station. It's nice to run against a cop with a sense of humor and I thanked him without too much sarcasm and left. My trusty drugstore phone booth was vacant when I dropped in and the directory gave me Dahlberg's number, which I got for a nickel. The man himself answered and I asked if he minded talking some and he said it was his favorite pastime and invited me over.

The house was modest almost to shy and he led me through a combination living/dining room to the kitchen, which was light and cheerful, and I got another cup of coffee and rolled a smoke with his permission. He lit up a Lucky and said shoot.

"What do you know about Delancy, the hardware man?"

"Well, he's pretty old, has a young wife, and no police record I can remember."

"You remember the partner he started the store with?"

"Vaguely. Seems like he and his wife died in a weird fire in their kitchen."

"Weird?"

"Well, I remember an old friend on the force who thought it wasn't quite natural but he couldn't make anything of it and there was no real investigation. Deal like that's damned messy."

By the time I'd finished my first cigarette I'd told him about

Rex Tobler's affair with Mrs. Delancy and my visit with her and the old man earlier in the evening.

"Well," he said. "You been busy. Must not get much sign painting done."

"Not today. This cop friend, he still around?"

"Retired two years ago. Lives across the street on the corner. Want to meet him?"

I did. He went and made a telephone call and then we walked to the man's house. It was dark and still out, the sky was all glittery with stars and the Milky Way made an almost solid path overhead. Someone across the alley called for Johnnie in a high, anxious voice.

The retired cop's name was Benson. He was bald, pugnosed, chunky, and spoke as gently as a loving mother in a voice that could lull a gorilla. The living room we sat in was dark shabby with tasseled lamps and antimacassars on the arms and backs of the couch and easy chairs.

He smiled ruefully when I asked about his suspicions at the time Delancy's partner and wife died in the fire.

"The whole setup bothered me. You see, the fire was pretty dandy for him—it got control of the store all to himself because the daughter, who was only seventeen, couldn't manage the place and trusted him. If I'd known at the time the old schemer'd marry the kid, I'd have really tried to push an investigation. It was all too much. But Chief McGlothlin said I was crazy and told me to forget it."

"What was weird about the fire?"

"It wasn't so much the fire itself, although I couldn't figure out how it happened, but the bodies were both by the table where they ate breakfast. I mean, you'd think one would've been by the stove maybe, or they'd tried to run from the kitchen, but no. There they were, sprawled by the table like they'd just sat there while the fire burned, then fell to the floor when it got to them."

"You ever hear anything about how smooth the partnership went?"

"Oh yeah. Delancy told me about it. Perfect pals. I asked around a little and couldn't come up with anything but didn't work much at it, to be honest, because McGlothlin's not a man you ignore."

"Well," said Dahlberg, "he's smart and he's the boss."

"He was the boss, all right," said Benson.

I could tell Dahlberg was bothered by the conversation when we left the house and we stood awhile at his front step going over it.

"One thing you got to remember," he said. "Benson always figured he should've been made chief when McGlothlin got it so there was never any love lost between them."

I said I'd keep that in mind and drove back to Greenhill.

20

A COOL BREEZE came through the hall Tuesday morning as I worked on the signs and it was so comfortable it seemed possible I'd make up for some of the time lost the afternoon before. When I heard steps on the stairway it didn't occur to me anyone but McGinty was coming up. When they stopped at the top of the stairs I turned and saw Rex Tobler was in the doorway, glowering at me.

From his expression he should have been carrying a gun or at least a baseball bat, but he was empty-handed.

"I wanna talk to you," he said.

"Have at it." I put my brush down and wiped my hands on a rag.

He stomped over and stood on the far side of the sawhorse table where I was working. His nose still had its sunshine glow but the eyes were dark and brooding under bushy brows.

"You went over to Norma's last night," he accused.

"I know."

"You didn't get anywhere."

"I got as far as I figured I would."

"What's that mean?"

"I know she can give you an alibi."

"What the hell kind of an alibi is it if we admit in front of God and everybody we were doing it in her old man's parlor? Everybody'll just figure she's covering for me because she went along with my killing Gen so I wouldn't have to marry her."

"Was Gen trying to make you marry her?"

"No, damn it, but that's what everydamnfool in town believes."

"You got a problem," I granted, and decided I'd better clean off my brush before it dried stiff. While doing that I went on. "Maybe the answer is you better help me figure out who else wanted Gen dead."

"How'd I know?"

"Let's figure some angles. You know where Norma was when her mother and father died in that fire at their house?"

"What's that got to do with anything?"

"I don't know. Tell me, maybe it'll help."

"She was at an overnight with girlfriends."

"The fire was in the morning?"

"Yeah. What the hell're you getting at?"

"I'm wondering about old Delancy."

He stared at me for a moment and his mad scowl faded into a confused frown.

"How well do you know him?" I persisted.

"Hardly at all. I never saw any percentage in getting chummy. Anyway, you're a mile off—he was upstairs in bed while I was with Norma the night Gen was killed—if he'd come down we'd sure as hell known it."

"Did you see him go up?"

"Course not. She didn't let me in until he'd gone up."

"Ever hear anything about him besides what Norma told you?"

"All I knew is he makes good dough and doesn't mind spending it on Norma and whatever she wants for the house."

"Did she say anything about how he got along with his partner at the store?"

"What're you getting at—you figure the old bastard was cagey enough to try and frame me for Gen's murder?"

"You got a better idea?"

"That's nuts," he said, but he liked the idea. "He's too damned old—never caught on—wouldn't want to catch on's long as the store made money and his wife took good care of him. And I told you, he was upstairs that night."

"Guys have been hired for jobs by old men with money who try to hang on to what's theirs—especially wives."

"Yeah? I never thought of that. . . ."

"Okay. Let's go over the guys. Your buddies. Which of them you think might've made her?"

"I dunno. Can't believe any of them could make her when I couldn't."

"Your buddy Dewey. He seems to've made out pretty good with the girls. How'd he manage?"

He shook his head reluctantly. "He never managed with Gen. She wouldn't take a drink. Old Dewey usually got them to have a little wine or gin and ginger ale. He didn't need that with Lorraine but I know he pulled that on a couple of girls he made."

"I hear your dad treated her good. How close you think he might have got?"

His face turned red and his voice went up. "I don't want to hear that kind of shit! He's too damned old—"

"Not that old, and you know it. He's good looking and not happy with his wife. And I know you've bitched that your old man treated his maid better than his son. Maybe it worked."

It cost him but he managed to tame his temper and shut up. When I asked about Mutt O'Keefe and Jim Baltz he was too shook to pay much attention. All he said, eventually, was they'd both been nutty enough about her to marry her, even if somebody else had knocked her up.

I asked if he thought Gen had big ideas and after sulking some more he managed to think about that and said yeah, he guessed she did. I kept after him, not pushing real hard, until he admitted that more than once, when he was trying to make out, she'd said she wasn't fool enough to let that happen and wind up pregnant unless she knew exactly where it would get her. And it sure wouldn't be as the wife of a guy who couldn't make a living.

"When I got real mad about that she tried to say she only said it trying to push me into making the most of myself. . . ."

"How soon after she said that was she killed?"

He scowled deeper than ever. "I guess a couple weeks—maybe a month. More like a month. I only saw her at the dance hall during that time—she wouldn't date me anymore."

"Did it scare her when you got mad?"

He looked embarrassed and nodded.

"Was she dating any of the other guys during that month?"

"I don't think so. If I remember right, she stuck close to the house."

"Okay. Now I've got to ask another question about your dad, and don't go flying off the handle, okay?"

He swallowed once and nodded but the flush came back in his face.

"Was he doing anything different around that time?"

He stared hard at me, trying to keep control, then looked down and took a deep breath.

"I remember he was running off to the cities a lot then. Had some big deal going on, I never knew or cared what the hell it was. Ma could probably tell you."

"Okay. Fine. Now how about you let me get back to work?"

"Uh, sure." He looked at me again and worked his face into a sincere expression. "But just one thing. Leave Norma alone, okay? Nobody's gonna nail me for killing Gen. There's no case and it's been too long and why screw everybody up over it now? You know I couldn't have done it, right?"

"I'm about convinced."

"Well, that's all I really wanted to say. See you . . ."

None of that gave me much satisfaction and I had a problem concentrating on the damned signs.

It seemed like the time for another chat with Marvel Tobler.

21

SPEED WICKERT WAS in a booth with Galbraith, the schoolteacher, when I drifted into the Do Drop Inn at noon, and waved me over.

"I'm off to Minneapolis soon's I finish breakfast," he announced.

"You eat it a little late, don't you?" I asked.

"Nah. I work late and play later, got to get my sleep in the morning."

"What do you do about classes and football practice during the school year?"

"Suffer a lot."

That got a laugh from Galbraith.

"What's the night work?"

"It isn't really nights—just afternoon and evening to maybe nine. I sell used cars for the Ford company downtown."

"And you drive a Chevy?"

"In a used car lot you sell all kinds—and this was a good deal—low mileage. Original owner was a little old blind lady so she didn't get out much."

Galbraith laughed again and I guessed that must be why they got along—Speed needed a straight man.

After ordering a ham on rye I looked at the teacher and asked if he'd been coaching at Greenhill High School when Speed played football there.

"I was. He made me look good."

"Not in English class," said Speed.

This time Galbraith didn't laugh. I looked back at Speed.

"It's funny—you selling Fords in Minneapolis and Rex doing the same thing in Aberdeen."

"Not funny at all—I started a year ago and we got talking last summer and I told him how easy it can be. Tried to talk him into coming to Minneapolis but he's got this little thing going in Aberdeen and couldn't see it."

Galbraith watched closely for my reaction, and I smiled at him.

"I guess you know about that," I said.

"About what?"

"The 'little thing' in Aberdeen."

"Oh, well, yes, I've heard. . . ."

I leaned against the booth back.

"The more I hear," I said, "the plainer it gets this town doesn't have any secrets. If that's so, then everybody already knows who killed Gen, so why're they keeping mum?"

"Because that's the one secret nobody wants to know," said Galbraith.

I looked at Speed. His grin fell somewhere between amusement and sympathy.

"You mean it's the need for everybody to pretend it couldn't be one of us?" I asked.

"You've pegged it," said Galbraith.

"Do they maybe approve of the murder?"

He shook his head firmly. "No. I don't believe that for a second. Genevieve may have offended a few people and aroused a great deal of envy among her classmates, but I'm certain no one felt she deserved death."

The waitress delivered my sandwich and I began eating. Speed and Galbraith were down to coffee by then.

"Are you supposed to be working in Minneapolis tonight?" I asked Speed.

He looked sheepish. "Yeah, but I'm not gonna make it. I called my boss and explained I had a little accident this weekend and would be a day late. Figure by another day the swelling will be mostly gone from my beak."

He left after wishing me luck and saying he'd see me. While I finished my sandwich Galbraith had more coffee and stayed on.

I asked him if there had been any town talk four years ago about trips Al Tobler made to Minneapolis.

He put his cup down after a sip and looked thoughtful.

"Yes, I believe there was. Al made a practice of hinting about big investments and mixing with important people. Someone reported he was checking into a dealership in the cities."

"Did he make any more trips there after Gen's death?"

"I'm not sure. It was at least four years ago. I can't claim I ever watched his moves that closely."

I drifted around to City Hall after leaving the café and found Schoop standing by his car in the bright sun, talking with an old-timer. The wind blew dust along the street and ruffled our hair.

I eased close and the old man took the hint and moved off after giving me a nod.

"You ever hear of Tobler trying to get a Ford dealership in the Cities?" I asked the cop.

He squinted against the wind and tried to look thoughtful. "You mean a while back?"

"Around the time Genevieve Sinclair got murdered."

"Ah," he said. "Let's get out of this sun."

We went into his office and he parked in his chair before the desk and I sat beside it, facing him.

"I seem to remember he was gone a lot that spring," he said, "but I didn't pay that much attention. Why you figure it's important?"

"I've been wondering if Mr. Tobler was planning a move out of Greenhill."

"Go on."

"Maybe he decided this town wasn't big enough for him. Especially if he left his wife and took his housekeeper along."

"I can't imagine Al being dumb enough to do that. Ever hear of the Mann Act?"

"Uh-huh. But if Al divorced his wife and married the girl, it'd all be legal."

"He sure's hell'd have to leave town if he planned that."

"You know if he made any more trips to the Cities after Gen's death?"

"No. But I guess we can dig into that. This could be a hell of a can of worms, you know?"

The telephone rang and he picked it up and growled hello. For several seconds he just listened while his eyes got wider and wider.

"Well, I'll be damned. Uh-huh. No question about who it is? Well, this kinda mixes it up, don't it? Yeah, matter of fact, he's right here. Wanta talk with him?"

He turned to me. "It's Officer Dahlberg in Aberdeen. He says they found a body in Delancy's backyard. He'd like you to come around and talk with him."

"Dutro?" I asked.

"Uh-huh. Looks like he got what Gen did. Ain't that a bitch?"

I got on the phone and told Dahlberg I'd be with him in about an hour. He told me not to drive over sixty. It surprised me he showed a sense of humor under the circumstances.

22

"WE DON'T KNOW for sure yet what did him in," said Dahlberg when I stopped in at the police station in Aberdeen. "My guess is he was clobbered from behind and then run over but the medical examiner'll have to make it official."

"How'd he turn up?"

"The guy playing gravedigger was lazy—only buried it a couple feet and a dog dug it up. Or was working on it when Norma Delancy looked out the kitchen window this morning and saw him digging and trying to pull something up."

"She identify him?"

"Nope. Wouldn't look. We got the landlady to do it but that was just a confirmation. Dewey's billfold was in his back pocket with his name and all. Body'd been there probably since last Wednesday night—didn't look too great."

"Whereabouts in the yard?"

"In the corner between the garage and the hedge where there's just bare ground because it gets no sun. Actually, all Norma saw was the dog's rear end when he was pulling like crazy on something she couldn't see and that made her nosy so she went out to look. A neighbor I talked with said we should've heard her scream clear to here."

Neither Norma nor Buff remembered unusual noises in their backyard that Wednesday night and they had spent the evening at home, listening to the radio. Norma claimed Buff had been dozing a good share of the time and they went to bed shortly after nine.

"Don't any of it make sense," Dahlberg complained. "Why the hell bury the body in Delancy's yard?"

"Well, it's a nice private spot. You talked with Buford?"

"Hell yes. He backed Norma up—said they listened to the radio, went to bed early—"

"Does he know his wife's been messing with Dutro's old buddy?"

"Why'd you ask that? Say he did know—what the hell reason'd he have to knock off Dutro and for God's sake bury him in his own backyard?"

"I'd like to know if he was wise."

Dahlberg didn't like any part of it but finally we got in his Ford and drove over to the hardware store. The boy I'd met before greeted us and when Dahlberg asked, said Mrs. Delancy hadn't come in this morning but the boss was in the back room. Dahlberg said we'd go back and talk with him.

Delancy seemed to have aged since I'd seen him at his home. The eyes were bloodshot, his hair tousled, and he'd had trouble knotting his tie straight.

Dahlberg leaned against shelving along the wall beside Buford's small desk and looked down at the old man sorrowfully.

"The trouble with murder," said the cop, "is it makes us have to drag out dirty laundry and look places we never'd think of poking any other time. You understand that, don't you?"

The old man stared up. His mouth sagged and his eyes were dull.

"Last Wednesday night, you and your wife Norma were home alone, right?"

That got a nod and a small frown.

"Nobody came visiting, that's what you said."

Another nod, a deeper frown.

"Just you and your wife together. I got to ask—do you two sleep in the same bedroom?"

The mouth closed and his Adam's apple bobbed as he swallowed hard.

"Why'd you ask that?" he croaked.

"I got to know were you together all the time."

The bloodshot eyes flickered my way, then back to the cop.

"We went upstairs together. She went to her room. I went to mine. The floors creak. If I got up, she'd heard me. Same both ways."

"She's awful young, isn't she? Like nearly fifty years younger'n you—right?"

"Not that much."

"You ever sleep together?"

The eyes lowered and the old man sighed. "We live like father and daughter. Clean and decent. I provide for her, she takes care of me. That was understood from the start."

"You know Rex Tobler?"

Buford looked up. The eyes were suddenly brighter. "Not well."

"You know he's been seeing your wife?"

That brought a sad smile. "That's a nice way of putting it."

"How much's that bother you, Buford?"

Buford straightened up and looked Dahlberg in the eye.

"I don't think about it. She'll stay with me because she's a good girl and knows I need her. So she's too young for me—if somebody can be nice to her and make her happy—all right. She don't run around with a crowd or get drunk or disgrace me or neglect me. Why'd I complain or fuss?"

"Don't you worry one day she'll go off with him?"

"Of course I do! You think I'm an idiot? So what should I do? Tell her she can't go out to movies or let him into the house after I've gone to bed? It's been going on for years—it goes on because I shut up and pretend it's not happening and so she stays with me and that's all I ask and we both understand and we don't talk about it. You think I mistook this Dutro fool for Rex Tobler and killed him and buried him in my own backyard? If you had a brain in your skull you'd arrest Rex—he's the one had a reason to kill that Sinclair girl—he's the one whose old buddy gave him an alibi he could give you idiots—he's the one who'd have a reason to kill that old buddy if he told you fools the alibi was all a lie!"

All this came in a snarling rush.

Dahlberg took all of it with no change in his sorrowful expression and at the end moved away from the shelving, glanced through the open door into the store, and turned back to Buford again.

"The trouble, friend, is Rex was with Norma the night that girl got murdered. There are at least three witnesses—not counting your wife. Now, I don't think you killed anybody. But I got to get all the facts I can to narrow this thing down, and believe me, none of this is any fun. It don't do no good for you to get mad at me and I'm not thinking you're a fool because of this thing with Norma. Get that out of your head."

Buford put his head down on the desk and started to bawl. I moved out into the store and drifted toward the street entrance, passing the young clerk, who was talking with a customer. Neither paid me any mind. After a little while Dahlberg came out and joined me.

"I wish," he said, "that you'd never come around. This job was fine till you did."

"Sure," I said.

"I suppose you think I sounded dumb—"

"You sounded fine. Real good. I never knew a cop who could've been better."

"I feel like a turd."

"You got no reason to. Now you ready to try Norma?"

He stared at me for a moment, then started toward his car. I went along and he didn't object.

23

I T T O O K A while before Norma finally answered Dahlberg's repeated knocking and at first I thought she'd been drinking. Her hair was mussed, her cheeks red, and her eyes bleary.

She apologized as she let us in, saying she'd not been sleeping nights, stayed home to rest, and had finally fallen asleep only a while before hearing us.

Dahlberg apologized back and she asked us to sit down while she started fresh coffee. She was too punchy at first to be curious about why we'd come around.

Drawn shades kept the room in deep shadows. The windows were open about six inches at the bottom and now and again a breeze edged through, stirring the drapes and keeping the air fresh. I saw a blanket on the couch where Norma had apparently been napping. Dahlberg and I took easy chairs and he sat staring at the fine carpet. I looked around. It was plain old Delancy was not a stingy man. The furniture was overstuffed and handsomely upholstered, the lamps were showy and numerous. They had the biggest radio I'd ever seen: a fancy cabinet job that was the attention center of the room, almost like a fireplace where they have them.

When Norma came back in she was still apologizing. Her cheeks were pink now instead of red and she had managed to tame her hair some.

"It'll be a minute yet," she said. "I must look a fright—"

"We been talking with your husband," said Dahlberg.

She lowered her round bottom to the edge of the couch and said, "Oh?" Her eyes became wary.

"He says you sleep in separate rooms."

"Why in the world would he tell you that?" A polite frown ended her apologetic spell.

"Because I asked. You mind showing us your rooms?"

"Whatever for?"

"Like I told your husband, this is a murder investigation. We got to know things that might sound nutty but just help us along, okay?"

She didn't like it. For a moment she stared at him, trying to dredge up something like a hostess's smile, then she rose and moved toward the stairway. We followed.

The floors did not creak.

"If your husband gets up in the night, can you hear him?" asked Dahlberg.

We were standing in her bedroom when he asked and for a moment she stared at him in astonishment.

"I don't believe this," she said. "Do you honestly think that old man got up in the night, went out and murdered a man, and buried him in his own backyard?"

"Ma'am, my business is to check everything and I'm doing what I got to do. Can you hear your husband if he gets up?"

"If he flushes the toilet, yes. If he killed someone in the hall I suspect I might've heard that but nothing woke me so I don't think it happened there."

She caught me grinning at her sarcasm and pretended she didn't.

"You ever meet this fella, Dewey Dutro?" asked Dahlberg.

She shook her head. "Rex never wanted me to meet any of his friends. He pretended they didn't know I existed."

"But you think they did?" I asked.

She gave me a direct stare. "I never knew a fellow who kept his love life a secret from his buddies."

"Did you know his friends brought him to your house the night Gen was killed?"

She was wide awake now and a look of resignation crossed her broad face. "Yes. I looked out the window because I was expecting him and saw the car and the fellows in it when he opened the door and got out. I didn't let on. He'd have been upset."

"Does he get sore at you a lot?"

"Only when I ask too many questions. He feels guilty because he has no plan for his life. He told me once he didn't know anything he'd want to do for a living. He said there wasn't a job in the world he'd want to stay with even a year. All he knows he wants is me."

"You ever meet his aunt?" I asked.

That got me a long examination.

"I just can't understand what any of this has to do with a body in our yard."

"We can't either until we poke into it," I said. "You visited her farm?"

"Yes, I did once. She was very nice to me. She's a lovely, lovely person."

"How'd Rex introduce you?"

"He said, 'This is my girl.' "

"You think Rex might want to run a farm?"

"I think he would, yes. He won't admit it. He pretends farmers are stupid but he likes to help out there and he loves hunting and just wandering around the fields. His aunt owns that farm— the people living there just take care of it and she pays them a certain share of whatever profit they make. His aunt was married a long time ago but her husband died when he fell off a horse. Farmers die in accidents a lot, you know."

I knew. It's a hazardous profession.

She said the coffee would be ready by now and we went down to try it.

"How'd you manage to get to the farm?" I asked.

"Buford was at a hardware dealers' meeting in Des Moines over a weekend so we had time."

"You think Rex took you there to see if you'd like a farm?"

"I suppose that was at least part of it. Then I thought he wanted me to meet his aunt and see how she'd take to me."

We drank coffee and were silent a moment before she sat forward and said, "I suppose you think I'm awful, being married to Buford and having a lover, but it's not as bad as it seems. Buff knows. I think he'd be upset if anybody else knew—but even that wouldn't crush him. If he can keep running his hardware store and have his house and me to care for it, nothing else matters all that much. He's not a proud man. He knows what he is and that satisfies him."

"You satisfied with things?" I asked.

"Most of the time, yes. I worry about Rex. I mean, not having to support me he just settles for us loving each other."

"How'd you feel if he wound up farming his aunt's land?"

"I wouldn't mind. It might be nice if rain ever came back to South Dakota. And if Buff died he'd leave me enough so we could get along until things got better. I'm afraid that's what Rex is depending on."

"Doesn't it worry you that Rex hasn't told you about any of his life? Like about what went on between him and Gen?"

"Well, that's not the sort of thing a fellow tells a girl he's trying to make love to."

"But you knew that he was a suspect in her murder; didn't you want to know why?"

"Of course. And he told me. They'd gone together at school

and necked some and she liked him better than the other fellows she dated. I imagine the other guys tried to make it sound like she was closer to him than any of them when they were scared after the murder."

She got up to pour more coffee and we were silent a moment while adding sugar and stirring. When she settled down again I said, "When I talked with you here last, you told me Rex hates his father and treats the servant better than his son. You think maybe the real reason he hates his father is he knew the old man was making out with Gen?"

She sipped from her cup and considered her answer before meeting my eyes once more.

"Will you promise not to tell Rex my answer to that?"

"Yes."

She looked at Dahlberg. "Will you promise the same?"

He nodded.

"All right. Yes, he knew his father made love to her. That he was the one who made her pregnant. He told me that when I insisted he be honest with me about what happened with that girl in their house. I was suspicious even before she was killed because it was so plain Rex hated his father and I couldn't believe it was just because he was bossy."

So, I thought, finally we're getting down to it.

24

I CAUGHT SCHOOP on his rounds Tuesday night about 9:30. He was in the pool hall and I must not have been wearing my poker face because he walked outside with me at once and asked what I'd learned that was new.

It didn't take long to cover. We were at City Hall by the time I finished and he suggested we get in his car and continue his rounds.

For a few minutes he was silent, then shook his head and began talking as he kept his eye on the graveled road.

"It all figures, but where does it leave us? He's got an alibi from Marvel. You know a woman can't be forced to testify against her husband—so why should she be able to testify *for* him?"

Never having had much time for guardhouse lawyers, I wasn't about to try being one and kept quiet.

He talked some of Al Tobler and it was plain he'd never liked the man and felt some qualms about trying to bring a case against him because he suspected a good many citizens knew his feelings and would figure he was prejudiced.

"And it'd scare old Jack S.," he said.

"From what you told me at the start of things, I thought that'd be just what the mayor'd want."

"Well sure, if it was all cut and dried, with us having Tobler dead to rights, but this way? No. And he wouldn't buy any notion of Al hiring the job out."

"What do you think Marvel'd do if she knew her hubby'd been diddling the hired girl?"

"I wouldn't ever pretend I knew which way Marvel Tobler'd jump no matter what. She's not the type you can figure anyway."

Picturing the fat woman jumping any direction was beyond my imagination but it was funny to think about. I shoved that idea from my mind and asked if he thought she could've done the job herself.

"If she worked out a foolproof plan, sure. And between us fellas, if anybody could do it, it'd be Marvel."

"How about we go around and talk to her?"

"Nah. He'd be home. I'd rather talk to 'em one at a time. We'll do it tomorrow. Her at home, him at the office."

As he dropped me off on Main I saw people coming out of the movie theater, spotted Prudence with her father, and caught up as they headed for home.

"How was the movie?" I asked.

Prudence said it was just fine, her father said nothing. I couldn't tell whether his implied disapproval was directed at the show or me. When we reached their front walk I halted and so did she. Her father gave us a nod and went into the house. Prudence took my arm and we walked up on the porch.

"I don't think your pop approves of me," I said.

"Well, he did warn me that you're a very experienced man, which I suppose means he thinks I'm too young for you. He admits you're probably more interesting than most guys I've known. He's also very shy and doesn't like to be in the way. Most of all, though, he trusts me and knows I won't do anything dumb."

I guessed her old man wasn't too dumb.

We sat on the wicker couch and she asked what I'd been up to—she'd heard I was out of town again.

I told her I'd been checking angles in Aberdeen.

"Have you got a girlfriend there?"

"No."

"Would you tell me if you did?"

"Probably. Does it make any difference?"

"I just wonder how hard you work at girl chasing."

"I never considered it work."

"No, I don't imagine. Did you get acquainted with Mrs. Delancy?"

"I talked with her. We didn't get cozy—I was with Officer Dahlberg."

"That must've been frustrating."

"Mrs. Delancy isn't like you think. Far as we can guess, she's never messed with anybody but Rex. Just between us, she and her husband don't sleep together. It's what folks call a marriage of convenience."

"So she's true to her husband in her fashion?"

"Right. I was surprised to see you at the movie with your dad."

"I talked him into it. Tried to get Mom too but couldn't. Movies get her too worked up when they're serious and she doesn't understand funny ones. She used to love Greta Garbo shows but had to give them up because she couldn't handle the tragedies."

We finally got around to a little smooching and then petting but she kept things well under control and I didn't try any wrestling. Finally she told me I was getting her too worked up and we should stop. I said I couldn't think of a poorer reason to quit but did when she insisted.

She went down the porch steps with me and we kissed again before parting. When she came up for air she pulled back a little and smiled.

"You're really very nice," she said.

"It's quite a handicap," I confessed.

She laughed and pushed me on my way.

25

BY EIGHT WEDNESDAY morning I was at work on the
signs again. The hall was cool and an easy breeze came through
the open windows so fine I didn't turn on the fan. Progress was
good until nine when Schoop climbed the stairs and suggested
we go visit Marvel Tobler.

I'd guess Schoop was the most sensitive cop I ever met. He
saw right off I was surprised he was inviting me along and told
me plain and simple the woman had always rattled him and it
would help him deal with her if he had some backup. I said I'd
be proud.

The next surprise came when the one who opened the door
after Schoop hit the bell was Rex. His mouth sagged a second
at the sight of us and he didn't offer to open the screen. If Schoop
was bothered he hid it well and said he wanted to talk with his
mother and while he was at it, with Rex too.

"What about?"

"If you can't guess you're not as smart as I think. You going
to let me in?"

"Why's he with you?" demanded Rex, scowling at me.

"Because I invited him."

That didn't satisfy Rex but after a second's pause he shoved the screen open and led us into the living room. We sat down while he went upstairs for Marvel.

"This is a break," Schoop said. "I've been wanting to talk with him."

I wasn't that sure. It seemed likely that Norma had called to tell Rex what she'd said to me and he'd rushed home to protect the fort. I told Schoop that.

Rex was gone long enough to convince me they were talking fast before joining us. Eventually they came down. Marvel's short hair was neatly combed, her mouth was lipsticked red, and her eyes were bright and challenging. The fact she didn't offer coffee, which is the first thing any Dakotan woman thinks of before liquor time, put us on alert this wasn't being accepted as a social call and she had no intention of pretending otherwise.

"I guess your son has told you what this is about," Schoop began.

"How would he know?"

"You mean he hasn't told you that his lady friend in Aberdeen told Carl here that your husband made Genevieve Sinclair pregnant?"

"Are you going to claim to believe what that woman told Carl?"

"Well, you can't hardly figure I wouldn't check on it."

"I'm surprised you'd take anything a woman like that would tell you as gospel. She's an admitted adulteress, a natural gold digger, and not very bright. And certainly couldn't offer any testimony an intelligent person would take seriously. Hearsay at best—"

"You're saying she can't believe what your son has told her?"

She looked at Rex. "Did you tell that woman your father made Gen pregnant?"

He was red and sweating. "I said he might've."

"Why in the world would you tell her a thing like that? Did you see them making love?"

"Gen told me he did."

"Why?"

"She was mad at me. We were out in the car and she told me we were through and I asked her if it was because of my father and she said yes, she was going to marry him as soon as he got a divorce because she was carrying his baby and she wasn't going to get stuck with any damn fool kid like me or my friends."

"Now," said Marvel, "there's more to this story. There's a reason she told him it was his father even though it was untrue. She told him because she'd learned from one of the gang of boys chasing her that they had a standing bet on who would get her cherry. When she learned that, she was crazy mad at all of the boys and she told each of them they'd never get it because she'd given it to a real man. And one of those boys killed her. It wasn't Rex and you know it because Norma has given him a solid alibi. It wasn't my husband because he was with me the night Gen was murdered. So you can just quit wasting our time and yours and concentrate on those fellows. For all I know it was probably Dutro and one of the other boys killed him out of anger and grief about what happened."

Schoop's jaw had dropped when she started that, but at the end he glowered at Rex and asked if there'd been such a bet. Without looking at his mother he nodded.

"That's pretty neat," I said. "Only now we have to figure out who had alibis for the night Dutro was killed. You got one, Rex?"

Rex turned redder than ever.

"You know where I was that night," he said to me. "At the dance here in Greenhill."

"Where'd you spend the night?"

"Here. In this house."

Schoop and I looked at Marvel, who smiled at us sweetly.

There didn't seem much point in asking if she'd back that up.

"Well," said Schoop, getting to his feet, "thanks."

He didn't think there was much point in calling on Al Tobler after all that but being stubborn and thorough he did it, and told me to go back to sign painting.

At noon I was having lunch at the café with McGinty when Schoop came in, took a booth, and waved me over. McGinty knew enough not to try joining us.

"He denies it all," Schoop told me after the waitress took his order and left us. "Claims he never screwed her. That she made the claim just to upset Rex because she was mad at him. I asked why was she sore at Rex and he said who knows why a girl gets mad at a boy? They just do. He also told me if I had a grain of sense I'd know damned well Marvel was too smart not to catch on if he'd tried anything like that and too mean to let him get away with it if he had managed to get into the girl's pants."

"He's probably level on that."

"So we're down to Mutt O'Keefe and Jim Baltz."

"Well, at least they're both in town and handy."

"Yeah, that's a hell of a comfort."

26

WE WALKED BACK to City Hall to get Schoop's Model A for a trip to the Baltz farm but were stopped on the sidewalk by Mayor Sullivan.

"Got a call from Aberdeen," he told Schoop importantly. "That Officer Dahlberg tried to call you but you didn't answer so he rang me."

"Why?"

"They got the autopsy done on Dutro. He was run over by a car. And they know whose."

"Yeah?"

"It was Delancy's Dodge. There's damage to the left fender and some blood. Delancy's in jail on suspicion of murder."

"They figured a motive?"

"Well, they say Delancy knew Rex Tobler'd been making out with his wife—figure the old man was trying to frame Rex."

"You mean Dahlberg figures Delancy used his own car to kill Dutro and then buried the body in his own yard and thought that'd frame Rex Tobler?"

"It's not Dahlberg's idea, it's the chief's. He thinks the old man's out of his head."

"Somebody is," said Schoop.

"Well, I'd think they must know what they're doing. And if so, everything's probably settled."

"You figure the old man knocked off Gen?"

"Of course not. This just eliminates any possibility that Rex killed Dutro to keep him from exposing his alibi. I think you'll just have to give up on the old murder."

Schoop scowled at the mayor's receding back and then glowered at me.

"Let's go see Baltz," I said.

"Might's well, what's to lose?"

But when we got to the farm we found only Signe Baltz and her husband home. She told us Jim had driven to Aberdeen to talk with someone about his teaching job in the fall.

"What'd he travel in?" I asked.

"The half-ton, what else?"

"I guess you've had that awhile."

"Six years, going on seven. My husband bought it. Never's given him a speck of trouble."

Schoop asked how her husband was doing and she said they'd had him walking yesterday, figured he might get down the stairs with a little help in a day or so.

Schoop wanted to go up and talk with him and she seemed pleased with the notion and led the way. The stairway was narrow and the hall likewise. It was more like a divided attic than two bedrooms but they'd fixed it up fairly well. There was no bathroom, only the outhouse. I guessed they took baths in a tub in the kitchen if they ever bothered.

Old man Baltz welcomed Schoop warmly enough and stared a little at me, which was nothing new in my experience. The missus brought a couple straight-back chairs for us to park on and Schoop asked questions about his progress and prospects.

"It's lucky your son could come around," said Schoop.

"I'd be even luckier if he was worth a damn on a farm," said Baltz. His wife let him know he was an ungrateful old grump and he quick asked Schoop how come he had nothing better to do than wander around visiting the sick.

"I figured I'd better make sure you were honest sick and hadn't been poisoned by your wife because you'd been getting cozy with the neighbor's daughter."

Baltz got a kick out of that but his wife didn't laugh or even smile.

"Actually," Schoop said, "I thought maybe we should talk about what happens when Jim goes back to teaching this fall and you're not in shape to run the farm."

"I don't guess that's any of your problem," said Baltz.

"My cousin Falwell'll help," said Signe.

"Some help," said Baltz. "He's useless as teats on a boar. But at least he won't always be running off somewheres."

"Jim make a lot of trips?" asked Schoop.

"Spends more time in Aberdeen than here."

"That right? Well, it's pretty much home for him now, isn't it? Happen he was there last week?"

"He was," said Baltz. His wife leaned forward and asked if he'd like some coffee. He shook his head but suggested she go get some for us. Schoop gave her his politician's smile. She didn't like it but got up and moved toward the stairs.

When she was out of sight Schoop asked, real casual, had Jim been in Aberdeen overnight a week ago.

"I don't know, I was muzzy then. Seems like he's been gone most of the time but that's probably just a notion. Signe says I can't forgive my son for being too smart to farm and that's hard to argue. You can't explain to a kid that farming's not always been like now. We had rain once—we'll more'n likely have it again and that makes all the difference. You know that."

Schoop said he did.

I said it was awful nice of Baltz to let his son use his truck for travel. Had he always let him do it? He said no, but Signe had. She never was able to say no to anything he asked.

Signe showed up with a pot of strong coffee and gave us cream and sugar to go along. There was no more talk of the truck but some general discussion of Jim and how smart he'd been in school. Eventually there was talk of Gen. Listening to Signe you'd think Jim had been the only boy the girl ever cared anything about and her death had been the greatest tragedy in Jim and Signe's life.

Jim, she told us, had been miserable and broody for months. Then he pulled himself up, turned ambitious, set off to school, and hadn't been seen much at home since.

"How'd he manage?" asked Schoop.

"Well, he got a part-time job at the biggest grocery store in town and I don't know quite how it was managed but it all worked out fine. He was able to satisfy the school he'd pay and they took him on because he had a great record at Greenhill High and Mr. Galbraith backed him all the way."

"Has Jim been interested in any particular girl since Gen died?" I asked.

"We don't really know. He doesn't talk about any, but to tell you the truth we kind of suspect it's a girl he goes back to see more than anybody he's dealing with about a job. I mean, he taught all last year and everything went fine so why'd there be a problem about this fall?"

We accepted that. Schoop asked some more general questions, and we drank our coffee and took our leave.

"Okay," said Schoop. "What you figure we got to make of all that?"

"I think we should find out exactly how Jim Baltz paid school expenses, who he's visiting in Aberdeen regularly, where he was a week ago tonight, and whether he had that family truck the night Gen was killed."

"Uh-huh. The first part's not bad. But finding out about the night four years ago, that could be hell to settle."

"You going to talk with Dahlberg?"

"I guess that's the only way. Let's go back to town and give him a call."

27

DAHLBERG TOLD SCHOOP that Chief McGlothlin was convinced Delancy had gone nuts. According to the medical examiner, Dutro had evidently been hit on the head with something like a tire iron before he was run over.

"Delancy denies everything," Dahlberg went on. "Says he always left his keys in his car so anybody could've taken it. Wife backs him up."

"What's the chief say about that?"

"He says it's what a man'd expect."

Schoop was so disgusted after hanging up he could hardly talk but finally passed on what he'd heard. I let him cool off before asking if the examiner, who looked at Gen four years back, found any head injuries. He said only a bruise on her jaw that might have come from a stunning blow.

"Did the car tracks tell anything?"

"Well, it looked like the driver'd been in and out of the ditch there. It was shallow, wouldn't give anybody a problem."

"So maybe she and the guy fought in the car—she got out, fell, and he ran over her?"

"I don't suppose we'll ever know," he said. "Not when we got that stupid chief involved."

"Where does Mutt work?"

"For his old man at the paper. Runs the linotype machine and does other stuff."

"Let's go see him."

He sighed, got out of his chair, and we headed downstreet.

Mutt's old man went in the back room and brought his son out when Schoop asked for him.

Before we could ask a question he asked one.

"You hear that old man Delancy's been nailed for killing Dutro?"

"Where the hell'd you pick that up?"

Mutt grinned. "I got a friend works on the Aberdeen paper. He was around City Hall and heard of it this morning. Did he have it right?"

"So we hear." Schoop glanced at Mutt's old man, who was standing by, listening, and suggested we take a short walk outside.

Mutt glanced at his father, who said go ahead, and we went out into the harsh sunshine and persistent wind. Schoop headed us around the corner where there was shelter from sun and wind and started his line.

"We heard a report from Mrs. Tobler this morning," he said. "She claims the guys who were giving Gen the rush back then had a standing bet that would pay off to the first guy who laid her. Is that right?"

Mutt's innocent face turned an angry red.

"That's baloney! We never did any such thing—why'd she say that?"

"Rex backs her up."

"He's a liar!"

"Could the guys have had such a bet and not let on to you?"

"I don't believe it. None of us ever talked about Genevieve like that. Never. Why'd Rex tell a lie like that?"

"I don't know. Maybe because his ma convinced him it would make a list of suspects. Guys who'd lose their temper and kill her when they found out she'd been had."

"That's the dumbest thing I ever heard."

"Okay. Fine. Mutt, did you ever have a chance to borrow somebody's car back in those days?"

"I didn't even know how to drive. My dad never owned a car till two years back and I sure didn't have pals who loaned out theirs."

"Okay. Don't get sore at me. I got to know these things to do the job—and you want the job done as bad as anybody, don't you?"

Mutt nodded miserably.

"I'd like to ask a question," I said.

They both looked at me. A citizen passed on the sidewalk and greeted Schoop, who raised his hand in greeting but didn't shift his eyes.

"You're a guy who pays attention to people, understands them; will you tell us which of the guys she was involved with was most important to Genevieve?"

He looked at a passing car in the street and then back at me.

"I'm not sure. Probably Jim. She figured he was the smartest of us and, I don't know, like, the most vulnerable. A couple times she called him 'poor Jim.' But I don't think any of us amounted to much except a little fun. She was more careful about stuff she said to him. Sometimes she'd make pretty mean cracks at Rex and she didn't mind treating me like a kid, but she didn't do that with Jim. It was like she had more respect for him."

He went back to work and we returned to City Hall, where Schoop called long-distance information and finally got hold of Speed Wickert. He denied ever hearing about the bet, admitted it could've gone on without him knowing, but didn't think it likely.

Schoop stewed awhile after that and couldn't think of anything but getting hold of Jim Baltz to question him about the bet.

"Fill me in on another angle," I said. "What'd Gen's parents tell you their daughter was doing earlier the night she was killed?"

"Gen's folks didn't know squat about what she did. She came and went as she pleased, spent most of her time over at the Toblers', and often as not met fellas she dated downtown. The night she was killed she'd done the cleanup at the Toblers' after their dinner and left about eight, according to Marvel. Rex had gone off with his friends earlier."

"She say how Gen and Rex had been getting on at the house?"

"If you believe Marvel, everything was hunky-dory. Al Tobler claimed the same. It was a normal night, hot, not too windy. Anyway—according to Gen's mother, Gen had come home after work, changed into a fresh dress, waved, and left. Nobody picked her up out front, she didn't say where she was going or how late she'd be. The only unusual thing her ma noticed was, instead of heading for downtown, Gen walked away from it, going south."

"So the killer picked her up on a street or maybe at the edge of town?"

"If he did, nobody reported seeing it happen."

"What'd the parents say of Gen's boyfriends? Did they know any of them, mention anything she said about them?"

Schoop crossed his legs and locked his hands behind his head.

"You know, that's the saddest part I remember about the investigation. Gen's ma and pa didn't know diddly damn about their own girl. She didn't talk to them about much of anything, never asked for favors. I got the feeling she didn't want to believe they were important any way or how. She'd like transferred her feelings outside and wanted to think she belonged with people

like the Toblers and her own folks were kind of an embarrass-
ment. They didn't tell me that, it's what I figured out talking to
them. I couldn't ever figure when Marvel was on the level but if
I got it straight, Gen treated her more like real family than her
own parents."

"Did Marvel claim Gen told her where she was going that
night?"

"No. Not that one or any other. About her own time, she was
independent as a hawk."

And that, I figured, was what killed her.

28

IN THE EARLY evening I found Steffi and Holly at the soda fountain and went in to join them. They asked for all the news I had about the discovery of Dutro's body and the arrest of the hardware man for murder.

Both pooh-poohed the arrest as too stupid for words.

"Well," I said, "it's a sad fact that a hell of a lot more murders are done by nuts and dumbbells than by masterminds."

"It's the nuts and dumbbells that get convicted," said Holly, "because there are a lot more simple cops than genius detectives."

I lifted my hands in surrender and admitted that both Schoop and I didn't think Delancy'd killed Dutro.

Steffi's eyes were bright with excitement and Holly had a slightly smug look because she knew she'd been clever.

"You don't believe the hardware man did it, do you?" said Steffi.

"No. Let me ask Holly a question. You ever hear of guys in your class making a bet on who'd be the first to go all the way with Genevieve Sinclair?"

Holly drew back. "No. Of course not."

"It's not likely you'd hear about it if they had, is it?"

"It'd depend. If Dewey was in on it, about everybody'd know."

"Did you ever date him?"

"No. It's not nice to say now, I suppose, but I never liked him. He was a bigmouth and sneaky. Tried to get girls drunk, and you know—"

"Who of the guys she ran around with do you think Gen liked best?"

"I'm not sure. She had a weird thing going with Rex, she teased him, made fun of him and said mean things, but she went with him quite a lot up until about a month before she was killed. I think she hoped sooner or later he'd show gumption and sense, start planning some kind of career, but he never did. She treated Mutt more like a little brother than a boyfriend. I think she really liked dancing with him because he had a way of showing off the girl he danced with. He'd twirl her around and let her dance like she was on her own at times. That's something Gen enjoyed, showing off. She'd wear skirts that showed her legs when she was spinning. Then she'd be pretty different with Jim Baltz. She liked dancing the slow pieces with him and they'd be real close and dreamy and, I don't know, she was sort of tender with him. Like she was afraid he was going to get hurt. He didn't make her starry-eyed or anything."

"How about the teacher, Galbraith?"

"She liked him an awful lot, but he was too afraid to encourage her and she gave up on him early. Gen wasn't a girl to waste her time."

"Did anybody make her starry-eyed?"

"I don't think she got that way. At least not in public."

"Were you ever in the Tobler house?"

"A couple times when I was a sophomore. That was the first year Gen worked for them and before she decided she didn't want me around too much."

"You ever notice how Al Tobler treated her?"

"No—I was only around once in an evening when he was home. They had a very big party for some people from other Ford dealerships and I was given a chance to help in the kitchen and even joined Gen in waiting on the table. I was too awed to be really observant but I remember Mr. Tobler was particularly approving of Gen and now I think of it, I guess I could say she was glowing that night. I can't say whether it was him or just the whole big affair. Everyone was very well dressed and there were candles and the silver was beautiful and the dishes handsome and there were flowers in big vases all around. It was very grand."

"How'd Al act toward you?"

"He was very nice."

"You told me he couldn't keep his eyes off you," said Steffi.

"I exaggerated," Holly said loftily.

"You said that's why Gen never wanted to be friends with you again."

"Well, that's how I felt at the time. I'm not so sure anymore. I suppose if I were honest I'd admit I was jealous of Gen, practically living in that nice house and being among all those fancy people."

"But he did have eyes for young girls," I said.

"Yes. But it wasn't offensive, somehow. He was so plainly admiring, almost approving, not at all like fellows on the street that leer at you. Not a bit."

"You notice anything about Marvel that night?"

"Only that she looked surprisingly smart for anyone so wide. She has a very intelligent and pretty face and her voice is wonderful and she's so quick."

"Did she keep an eye on her husband?"

"I'm sure she did but with her it was never obvious. I'm just certain she'd not miss the slightest thing."

"Did you know Gen's parents?"

"Way back, yes. They're sweet. They just lived for Gen and she didn't have a lot of time for them. One thing's for sure—she never washed a dish or cooked an egg at home, let alone did any dusting or the like. They treated her like a visiting princess, not a daughter."

"How do you think they'd react if you and I went over to visit this evening?"

"What for?"

"I'd like to ask them a few questions. Maybe you being along, an old friend, would make it easier."

"What kind of questions?"

"Whether she ever said anything about her guys, maybe dig a little to find out about her last night at home."

"I think that might be cruel."

"It might be—but it also might not hurt for them to know somebody still cares enough to be trying to find out what really happened."

"Go ahead," said Steffi, "don't be chicken."

Holly gave her a look that was supposed to wither the little sister but made absolutely no impression. Then she said all right, let's do it.

29

THEIR NAMES WERE Mae and Morley Sinclair. Mae answered Holly's gentle knock, greeted her warmly, and when Holly had introduced me and asked if we could talk with her, said of course, do come in. The front door opened directly on their small living room and I saw a grizzled old man sitting on the edge of a battered easy chair at a card table under a floor lamp that showed a game of double solitaire under way. He scowled at me through shaggy eyebrows.

"I was wondering if you'd ever make it," he rumbled.

"He's been busy," said Mae, smiling at me with plain approval. "Why don't you two sit on the couch? I'll do coffee—"

I tried to tell her that wasn't necessary but she knew better and went into the kitchen. Morley scrooched back into the easy chair as we sat down.

"What'd you do before retiring?" I asked him.

"Worked at the grain elevator. Weighed the loads, figured the pay, did all the work the manager got paid for. You going to find out who killed our girl?"

"Hard to say. It was a long time ago."

"Like yesterday to us. Always will be."

"You got any ideas?"

"It's time you asked. I'll tell you who did it. That Al Tobler son of a bitch. He's the only one could've got her pregnant. She was too smart for all those boys she ran around with, but Al, he's smooth as green grease, he'd manage a young girl easy as I'd pat a dog."

He jerked his head toward the kitchen.

"She won't believe that. Won't believe anybody'd do it on purpose. Had to be an accident and the guy driving went off in a panic. But it was pretty handy for Al, wasn't it? Because Gen wasn't a girl'd let him get away with making her pregnant and keeping her mouth shut like Hester in *The Scarlet Letter*."

"You remember how Gen was feeling the last weeks she was alive? Was she worrying or—"

"She was floating. You never saw a girl more happy than Gen. That's a thing sustained us. We like to think she died so quick she was still happy."

"So she had plans. Didn't she give any hints what they were?"

"No. We can only guess she was excited about the baby and thought she was going to get its father. I told her once she looked like the cat that ate the canary and she laughed and said maybe she had but that's all. She was always leaving, it seems like. Never saw her but a few minutes or so. Always on the run. It's hard to believe she'll never run again. . . ."

His voice choked off and he turned to hide his watering eyes as Mae came back from the kitchen.

"Coffee'll be ready in an instant," she assured us. "I can offer you cookies or doughnuts."

I sighed and said doughnuts. Holly smiled.

Morley got up from his chair, went into the kitchen, and I heard water running in the sink.

"Did Gen ever talk about the Tobler family to you?" I asked Mae.

"She didn't talk much about anything else. She thought they were all wonderful. I asked her once, if that was the case, how come she went with so many boys besides Rex? She said that way he didn't get tired of her."

"Did she ever say anything about the stories of Al Tobler working on some deal in Minneapolis?"

"I asked her about that once and she told me not to give it a thought. Naturally that got me wondering what she'd do if the family did move to Minneapolis and when I asked her that she told me I was the one who always was saying don't go looking for things to worry about, they'll find you when it's time."

"You don't have any idea where she was going that last night?"

"No. She came home about 8:30 from the Toblers', went to her room, changed clothes, came out, said good-bye, and was gone."

"Did she dress up or down?"

"Well, she never really dressed down. I'd say she just put on a fresh frock, to make her feel new, you know?"

"Was she excited?"

"It's hard to tell, thinking back. I had the feeling she was maybe a little more thoughtful than usual. Like she had something important on her mind."

"Did you ever happen to notice if she dressed any differently depending on the fellow she was planning to see?"

"Well, there was a pretty clear difference between what she wore at the Toblers' and what she put on for dates. At the Toblers' she wore things a little more older like. Heels, you know? And not such bright colors."

"Was she wearing heels that night?"

"No. I mean, not high. Casual, you'd say."

"I understand she wasn't dating Rex that last month. Was she still seeing Mutt, Jim, or anybody else?"

"She wasn't seeing Mutt all that much, or Jim. I think she

worried some about Jim. He was a serious boy, you know. Got the best grades of any boy she knew and took things very seriously. I remember her calling him 'poor Jim' a couple times. He felt guilty about not working on his father's farm and his father didn't make things easy. Complained a lot."

I could imagine that.

"Did any of the fellows who'd been after Genevieve ever come around to see you after she died?"

"Why yes," she said, brightening. "Jim Baltz came. He showed up the night before he left to go to school and told us there had never been anybody like her and there never would be and we should be proud because she thought the world of her mom and dad and he wanted us to know. Wasn't that nice? All three of us wept, didn't we, Morley?"

He nodded and stared at the solitaire game on the table before him.

"He ever come around again?"

"No. But he wrote a letter a couple years back. He said if we heard he was seeing a girl in Aberdeen he wanted us to know that Genevieve was still the only one that was his true love and he wanted us to know he'd not forget her no matter what happened in his life."

She went into the kitchen and returned with coffee and doughnuts and we gabbed some more, but all the new I learned was almost anybody makes better doughnuts than my ma.

30

"DID YOU GET anything from that?" Holly asked as we walked back toward her house.

"Maybe."

"What?"

"Not sure enough to talk about it."

Steffi was sitting on the front porch steps when we arrived and wanted filling in on all we'd learned. Neither of us gave her any satisfaction and that annoyed her enough so she kept hanging around even when Holly told her to go to bed.

When I left they were still arguing.

I got to the edge of town in no time and stood awhile, looking across the prairie stretched under the clear sky and glittering stars to the dark black rim where there was no light, and thought about Jim Baltz and Gen Sinclair.

I went back to the hotel, started my Model T, and headed for the Baltz farm. Light was visible in the kitchen the moment I topped a small rise about a quarter of a mile from the farm and I figured it meant what I expected.

It did. The half-ton truck was parked in the side yard. I let my lights hit the house, pulled up beside the truck, killed the motor, and sat a moment. The back door opened and Jim came out moving slow and thoughtful.

We met half a dozen yards from the back steps.

"How'd you know I was home?" he asked.

"Didn't know. Thought it was possible. I've been talking with the Sinclairs."

"Oh? Mind if we walk a ways from the house? Dad sleeps light and I'd rather not wake him."

We moved out to the barn and while he leaned against the wall and stared up at the sky, I rolled a cigarette.

"So," he said, "what'd Mae and Morley have to say?"

"That Gen liked you best of all the boyfriends. Figured you were smarter, more sensitive than the others."

He watched the flame as I lit my cigarette. The flare made a sharp sound in the night that was silent except for crickets, carrying on steady as women's voices at a Ladies Aid supper.

"Is that all they said?" he asked.

"They said that evening, before she was killed, Gen seemed real thoughtful and serious. Like maybe she was going to be saying good-bye to someone."

So I stretched the truth a little.

"What'd you make of that?" he asked, looking at me.

"I'd guess it was because she was on her way to her last date with you. She was deciding how to handle it so you wouldn't be hurt because you were the one guy she really cared about."

He went back to watching stars.

"I'd like to go over with you what I figured happened," I said.

He took a deep breath, let it out, and said, "Go ahead."

"I think she started off things letting you kiss her and do what you wanted, because she was already pregnant and there was no reason to hold you off anymore. After you'd made love I figure she told you this was your last time together and she'd wanted to make it important, and then said she was going to marry Al Tobler, who was going to get a divorce, marry her, and take her to Minneapolis. You got mad and there was a fight, she jumped out of the truck cab, and you ran over her. I think you lost your head for a few minutes because for you she'd been the perfect girl and all of a sudden you knew she was a scheming, greedy woman who wanted it all and she let you in because she wanted to be remembered as your all-time big moment."

He stared at me, his eyes wide and his face haggard.

"Several people," I went on, "said you were the one young guy Gen really respected and wouldn't want to hurt. And it's pretty certain Rex couldn't have killed her, neither could his father. Al Tobler really intended to walk out on his wife and take over a dealership in Minneapolis. He didn't have any motive for killing her."

Mention of the Toblers changed his expression from suffering to anger. He scowled at me.

"What if he wasn't going to get that dealership in Minneapolis? What if it wasn't as easy as he thought and he decided he couldn't divorce his wife without her getting all his money so he told Gen to get an abortion and promised to pay for it but she said nothing doing?"

"That's not a bad theory. I'll check it out. But if that's not the case, your only defense'll be your mother's word that you were home the night Gen was killed. You want her to lie for you after she's sworn to God she's telling the truth, and maybe get nailed for perjury?"

"How'd she get caught for that?"

"Once a trial starts you never know what'll come up—witnesses that saw things you didn't realize, people with grudges—hell, anything can happen. And how about the night Dutro was killed? You got an alibi for that?"

"I heard they already arrested Mr. Delancy for Dutro's killing."

"They'll have to nail him in court and they'll never make it.

One look at that old bird tottering up to the witness stand and a few words from him in testimony—that's all it'll take for him to walk out clean."

He'd switched from stargazing to dirt watching and I couldn't see his expression in the dark shadows but his shoulders were hunched as if he were in pain. I tried another tack.

"Your ma knows you did Gen, doesn't she? That's why she egged you into siccing me on Rex Tobler. She figured the Toblers were to blame for the whole mess and she wanted them to sweat for it."

He stared at the house and whispered, "Oh God . . ."

"Did you shove Gen out of the car, or did she pull loose and jump out screaming and you ran over her to make her quiet?"

"It wasn't like that! Nothing like that at all! It was an accident. Part of what you said's right—she told me where to drive and there by the cemetery told me she wanted me to make love to her and I was so excited and happy I about died.

"She said it had to be done right and asked if the seat in the cab came out and I said yes and she said put it in the bed of the truck and we'll do it there. I was scared, thinking what if a car came by, but she said don't worry, drive into the ditch a little under the trees there and I did.

"Afterward, we lay there close and she told me she hoped I'd understand that was our last time together. At first I couldn't believe what I was hearing. She said she had to plan her life so she wouldn't be a poor nobody like her mom and dad, she wanted to be somebody and she had this chance. I was too flummoxed at first to really understand what she was saying but when she said she was pregnant by Al Tobler it all came down on me. I was just stunned. And then I started getting mad that she had done this, just being kind to me like I was some dumb plowjock. I mean, it was goddamned condescending. I started yelling. I told her she was a dumb whore. She got mad back and tried to get up and I grabbed at her, still yelling, she swung on me, kneed me, and tried to climb out of the truck bed. I caught her foot trying to pull her back but only tripped her up and she fell to the ground and rolled into the ditch. I went to her and she just huddled up there and told me to go to hell, she hated me.

"I got into the truck and started it but had left it in gear and it jerked back and ran over her. I'll hear that scream till I die. I panicked and pushed the truck into first and felt it go over her again. I was crazy by then. I killed the engine, got out, and went to her but she wasn't breathing and I knew she was dead.

"I got back in the goddamned truck, drove home, looked the truck over to be sure there was no sign of what'd happened, and went to bed. I heard her scream all night, and every night. I always will. . . ."

I let him stew in that for a while as I rolled and lit another cigarette.

"It's too bad you had to go and kill Dutro," I said. "With just Gen, it might've gone down as manslaughter, maybe even lighter."

He laughed bitterly. "That's the funniest part—I didn't kill Dewey. Never ever even thought of it. If it wasn't old man Delancy it was somebody else—maybe his wife. But it sure as hell wasn't me. I was in a whorehouse that night near the depot in Aberdeen. But you know what a whore's testimony's worth."

I said I'd check the place out and if anybody backed him up it might help even without court testimony.

He stood silent for several seconds and finally looked at me square.

"You can't prove any of this," he said.

"Maybe not. You think you can just forget it all?"

He looked toward the house. I thought I saw movement in the kitchen but no one came to the door to look out.

"I'm going in now," he said.

"Why not go back to town with me, talk with Schoop?"

"No. I'll talk with Ma. Maybe I'll come to town in the morning. I got to think."

"Okay," I said. "I hope you can sleep. Good night."

He was slowly walking toward the back door as I pulled out and headed back to Greenhill.

31

WHEN I PULLED up in front of City Hall Schoop was standing in the front entrance.

"Think I've got something for you," I said.

"Shoot."

I told him of my talk with Jim Baltz.

"And you went off and left him at the farm?" he asked.

"Uh-huh."

"Great. And what if he takes off, or shoots himself, or just decides we can't prove shit, goes back to Aberdeen, and says the hell with it?"

"I think there's something else he'll do."

"Like what?"

"Kill Al Tobler."

He stared at me for a moment. "Because he got Gen pregnant and caused all that happened after? Yeah. Let's head over to the house."

We decided to hike the four blocks, leaving our cars in front of City Hall. After casing the house he said he'd watch the front while I covered the back. There were large pine trees in front and he used them as a screen. I moved into the lilac hedge along the alley. We figured either Jim would try to get Al out to meet with him someplace, or he'd try sneaking into the house, figuring it wouldn't be locked on a hot summer night and he could find his way to the master bedroom.

Nearly an hour passed with nothing happening but crickets chirping and an owl hooting somewhere in the distance. Didn't even hear a dog bark. The moon was three-quarters full and bright enough to throw sharp shadows and all the sky away from it was sparkling with stars. A lot better night for loving than murder.

I heard the truck engine first and looked for its lights but they weren't on. It idled up snug against the dense brush of the lilacs near me on the alley side. I'd been sitting on the ground when I first heard the motor and quick got my feet under me before it was shut off. There was a moment of silence so profound I could hear the pings of the cooling engine. Then the door opened and closed with a small squeak and I heard footsteps go around to the truck bed, then start toward the opening in the lilacs.

The dark figure walked through a puddle of moonlight before disappearing in shadows made by a big oak in the side lawn. He was carrying a large, round metal gasoline can with a handle.

He reached the back stoop, paused, and looked around. I stayed frozen. Then he bent over the can. I heard the cap turn as he unscrewed it and then a gurgle as he started splashing the contents on the door and across the stoop. I let him get to the corner, still sloshing gasoline against the house, stood, and started for him. He was so intent he didn't notice my rush until I was within diving distance and only managed to straighten up slightly before I drove my shoulder into his side just above the hip. He grunted and slammed against the house, the can crashed against base blocks, and I rolled free before he could recover enough to grab for me. I saw his hand go for a pocket and kicked it. His yell of pain was enough to hurt my ears and then I was sitting on him and Schoop came charging around the corner and dropped to his knees at my side.

"Check the right pocket," I said, "he's got matches or a lighter there."

In a second Schoop had the matches and we dragged Jim to his feet.

"Well," said Schoop, "you figured on getting the whole family. You think that'd make everything okay?"

Jim clutched his arm with his left hand, shook his head, and said I'd broken his wrist. And that's all he said through the doctor's exam, the setting of the broken bone, and the questioning we tried to do after. Finally we left him in the cell. I went back to the Fuller Hotel and hit the sack.

32

I WORKED ON signs in the hall through the morning. McGinty showed early and wanted the gory details since the word was already around about Jim Baltz being arrested. He told me Signe Baltz had been over at the courthouse talking with her son and had a lawyer coming from Aberdeen, some sort of shirttail relation.

A little before noon I knocked off and went to the courthouse. Schoop was there, looking as if he hadn't slept in a week. He said he'd been talking with Signe after she'd visited with her son.

"That's a hell of a strong woman," he told me. "No bawling or wailing, no tears or threats. She says he did it, he'll admit it and take his medicine."

"Wait'll the lawyer gets here," I said.

"I'm not waiting. We're gonna talk with him, okay?"

I agreed. He got Jim from the cell and brought him into Schoop's two-bit office.

Jim quietly told Schoop everything he'd told me the night before, only this time he elaborated on how Al Tobler had seduced Gen. Al did it with sweet talk, careful moves, and a few million promises over a year's time. He talked about Minneapolis and St. Paul, a car of her own, trips to California, Florida, and even Europe. The wooing, according to Jim's report of Gen's story, was a rare combination of romance and materialism. She had been convinced Al Tobler would make her a queen.

The whole business, Jim insisted quietly, had driven him out of his mind but that had not made him a murderer, it simply made him lose control so he said things that made Gen lose her temper and caused their fight, which ended in his accidentally running over her.

"What about Dutro?" asked Schoop.

"All right," he said. "I'll tell you about that. Dutro took money from Al Tobler to give Rex his alibi. And later he decided he could maybe make a little more out of his advantage when he realized how screwed up the Delancys would be if he told what he knew about Rex's involvement with Norma. He called old man Delancy—"

"How'd you know this?"

"Dutro told me. Only in the midst of things he found out that Doozy Knight had blabbed about being with him and decided he better move quick. He called Delancy and explained he needed a little loan to cover expenses for a trip to California and the old man agreed and told him to come over Wednesday night. I saw Dutro after he had his date with Myra Payne. We had a couple beers together and he said if I ever made it to California, look him up, and that was it. I assumed after that he got his money and lit out. Until the body showed up. I didn't figure it would do me any good to get involved so I kept quiet. Fact is, I pretty much figured Rex must have done it; I couldn't imagine the old man or Norma doing him. Especially when the body was in Delancy's yard. So that's it."

Schoop worked on him awhile without developing anything more and finally took him back to his cell and we sat going over it all.

"I know it chokes you up," I said, "but it looks like the old man did it, buried him quick, and maybe planned to move him later. Or maybe he was shrewd enough to figure ahead that nobody'd think he'd be dumb enough to leave the body in his own yard after running over it with his own car and Rex'd get blamed. Remember the retired Aberdeen cop who was convinced the old man knocked off his partner several years back? If he did and got away with it, he probably figured he was cute enough for another caper."

"We haven't got a prayer of going back and proving he killed that couple."

"Maybe not. But why not talk with Norma, go over things she remembers, see if along the way you can't make her realize what the old bastard pulled on her. If he actually did kill them she ought to remember things that would cinch it once she puts her mind to it. The only word about how great he got along with Norma's parents is what he's given us himself. What's needed is, we get the Aberdeen cops to poke around and get somebody else's view of how it was."

I finished the last sign early Friday afternoon and Mayor Jack Sullivan paid me off when I reported to his office. He told me I'd done a wonderful job and I thought he meant in helping to solve the killing but it turned out he meant on the signs. I took the money and what satisfaction I could from his approval and went to visit Schoop. He told me things were going fine in Aberdeen. He'd had a couple long talks with the chief there, who was satisfied that he was right about Delancy being Dutro's killer and wasn't worried about the details. His men had already found witnesses who said here had been bitter relations between Delancy and his partner and it seemed likely they'd manage a conviction.

I stayed over Saturday to take Prudence to the dance and

got in rounds with Holly and Steffi on the dance floor. Unfortunately that's as far as I got with any of the women in Greenhill. Prudence didn't even let me get as far as I'd gone the Saturday before.

She wrote me the letter she promised our last night. It came to the Wilcox Hotel in Corden where I picked it up when I went back for Thanksgiving.

She said things were dull with me gone but didn't suggest it was quite unbearable. She said old Delancy had a stroke the second day of his trial and died that night. Rex and Norma were getting married in the spring and Rex was going to take over for the couple who'd been running his aunt's farm with the understanding she'd make it his if he wanted to stay on.

"Poor Jim was convicted of Gen's murder. It's so sad because if he hadn't tried to set the Tobler house on fire I don't think the jury would have settled for anything more than a manslaughter charge. There are still lots of people in town very bitter about the way Gen got treated by the defense in the trial where they made out she was a terrible schemer and flirt. I suppose it will wear off eventually. Al and Marvel Tobler are moving to St. Paul, where he's taking over a car distributorship. Stories about his involvement with Gen haven't exactly improved his business around here so he decided to go. Some of us were surprised Marvel went along. Maybe she plans to make him pay on the long haul.

"Steffi sends her best—and Holly has moved to teaching school in a suburb of Minneapolis called Edina. I understand it is all full of rich kids. Which would suit Holly just fine.

"I'll close on that catty note—and hope you'll come back to Greenhill in the summer."

I figured I would.